THE ADVENTURES OF THE PUZZLE CLUB

And Other Stories

THE ADVENTURES OF THE PUZZLE CLUB

And Other Stories

BY ELLERY QUEEN
& JOSH PACHTER

Crippen & Landru Publishers
Cincinnati, Ohio
2022

For information contact:

Crippen & Landru, Publishers

P. O. Box 532057

Cincinnati, OH 45253 USA

Web: www.crippenlandru.com

E-mail: Info@crippenlandru.com

ISBN (softcover): 978-1-936363-66-7

ISBN (clothbound): 978-1-936363-65-0

First Edition: October 2022

10 9 8 7 6 5 4 3 2 1

TABLE OF CONTENTS

Introduction
By Josh Pachter

Before I turn my attention to Ellery Queen, I'd like to begin with Agatha Christie.

Dame Agatha's Jane Marple was introduced to readers in six short stories about the "Tuesday Night Club," which appeared in six consecutive issues of the monthly *Royal Magazine* from December 1927 to May 1928 and were collected (with seven later Marple stories) as *The Thirteen Problems,* published in the UK in 1932 and in the US (as *The Tuesday Club Murders*) in 1933. The Tuesday Night Club was a group of six people—including former Scotland Yard commissioner Sir Henry Clithering—who met once a week for six weeks at Miss Marple's home in the village of St. Mary Mead. In each story, one member of the group recounted a "real-life" mystery—each, of course, invented by Christie and *not* "real life" at all—which the other five attempted to solve. And each week it was the dithery Jane who saw her way to the mystery's solution.

Thirty-seven years later, Ellery Queen—I told you I'd come to him!—introduced the Puzzle Club in a story titled "The Little Spy," which appeared in *Cavalier*'s January 1965 issue. A second story, "The President Regrets," followed eight months later, in the September '65 issue of *Diners Club Magazine.*

It seems likely that Frederic Dannay and Manfred B. Lee, the cousins who wrote together as Ellery Queen, quickly tired of the concept. Whether their Puzzle Club was a conscious or unconscious imitation of Christie's Tuesday Night Club or only coincidentally similar to it, they didn't return to it for six years.

In 1971, though, three more stories appeared in quick succession: "The Three Students" and "The Odd Man" in, respectively, the March 1971 and June 1971 issues of *Playboy* (of all places!), and "The Honest Swindler" in the Summer '71 issue of *The Saturday Evening Post.*

Why did they end the series there, before producing enough Puzzle Club stories to fill a book?

I haven't seen any of the various EQ biographers or other scholars address this question, but I note the following:

- It's generally acknowledged that, while Fred Dannay was the plotter in the EQ partnership, Manny Lee did the lion's share of the *writing.*
- Manfred B. Lee died on April 3, 1971.
- The final Ellery Queen novel, *A Fine and Private Place,* was published in 1971. (One additional novel, *The Blue Movie Murders,* came out in '72, but it featured Mike McCall, not Ellery, and though credited to "Ellery Queen" it was ghostwritten by Edward D. Hoch.)

Given these facts, I conclude that the Puzzle Club died with Manny Lee in 1971.

Ten months later, "The Acquisitive Chuckle"—the first entry in Isaac Asimov's long-running series of tales of the Black Widowers—appeared in the January 1972 issue of *Ellery Queen's Mystery Magazine.* It would be followed by another sixty-five stories, most of which were published in *EQMM.*

Conventional wisdom has it that the idea for the Black Widowers came from the Trap Door Spiders, a literary dining club Asimov belonged to, but I find it hard to believe that the birth of Asimov's puzzle-solving dinner club following so close on the heels of the death of the co-creator of Ellery Queen's Puzzle Club was coincidental.

Compare the memberships of the two groups, and the possibility of coincidence becomes, at least in my opinion, remote:

The six members of the Puzzle Club included Ellery Queen (a mystery novelist), Darnell (a criminal attorney), Dr. Arkavy (a biochemist), and Emmy Wandermere (a poet), while the six members of the Black Widowers included Emmanuel Rubin (a mystery novelist), Geoffrey Avalon (a patent attorney), James Drake (a chemist), and Mario Gonzalo (an artist). The only two members who *don't* overlap are the Puzzle Club's Cyrus Syres (an oilman) and Dr. Vreeland (a psychiatrist) and the Black Widowers' Thomas Trumbull (a cryptographer) and Roger Halstead (a high-school math teacher). In addition to the two clubs' official memberships, the Black Widowers also had Henry Jackson, the waiter (who solved the mysteries), where the Puzzle Club had Charlot, host Syres' chef (who cooked the dinners but did *not* solve the puzzles).

It seems unavoidable to conclude that—though Asimov may well have belonged to a literary dining club called the Trap Door Spiders—his Black Widowers were to at least some degree a replacement for Dannay and Lee's Puzzle Club.

Q, as Ellery himself might have said, ED.

Okay, now that I've gotten that off my chest, let's move on, shall we?

In the early 1970s, not long after Manny Lee's death, I suggested to Fred Dannay that he edit a collection of EQ pastiches, parodies, and other homages to be titled *The Misadventures of Ellery Queen.* Fred liked the idea, but didn't feel it would be appropriate for him to compile such a volume himself and invited *me* to do it. Almost half a century later, with the approval and encouragement of the Frederic Dannay Literary Property Trust and the Manfred B. Lee Family Literary Property Trust, I did.

Well, when I say "I," I actually mean "we." Echoing the Dannay/Lee partnership, I co-edited the book with a partner, Dale C. Andrews, a Queen *pasticheur par excellence* I met through our mutual friend Francis M. ("Mike") Nevins. For a period of two years, Dale and I steeped ourselves in the worlds of Queenian pastiche, parody, and tribute—and somewhere along the line I found myself itching to write a pastiche of my own.

The result was "A Study in *Scarlett!*", a further adventure for Ellery and the Puzzle Club, which I sent to *EQMM* editor Janet Hutchings—who agreed to buy it for the magazine with the caveat that it would be a one-off, not the *kick*-off for a series of Puzzle Club pastiches.

I hadn't originally thought of "*Scarlett!*" as being anything *other* than a one-off, but the moment Janet cautioned me not to do a Puzzle Club series I began to think that it would actually be a lot of fun to *do* one. There really isn't any other market for Queen-derived fiction beyond *EQMM,* though—and, when it comes to *EQMM,* Janet is the boss. So I responded to her email with a promise that I wouldn't submit any follow-ups ... although, I said, that was a shame, because it would be fun to do a total of five of them, to bookend the five originals.

And Janet wrote back to say, basically: *Well, if you promise there'll be only five, and if you'll space them out and not send them in too close together...*

I was happy to promise, and the Dannay and Lee heirs gave me their seal of approval, so I set to work.

As you have perhaps recognized, the title for my first Puzzle Club story—which appeared in the May/June 2019 issue of *EQMM*—was a pun on the title of Arthur Conan Doyle's first Sherlock Holmes work, *A Study in Scarlet,* which appeared in the 1887 edition of *Beeton's Christmas Annual.*

If I were going to write four more stories, I decided, I ought to use Sherlockian puns for *their* titles, too—and it was a short step from that to the decision to continue using puns on Sherlockian titles that mentioned colors. So I went through the three remaining original Holmes novels and the fifty-six short stories, looking for colorful titles. There turned out to be more of them than I would have guessed, especially if you stretch the definition of the word "color" just a bit: "The Red-Headed League," "The Five Orange Pips," "The Adventure of the Blue Carbuncle," "The Adventure of the Beryl Coronet," "The Adventure of the Copper Beeches," "The Adventure of Silver Blaze," "The Adventure of the Yellow Face," "The Adventure of Black Peter," "The Adventure of the Golden Pince-Nez," "The Adventure of the Red Circle," even "The Adventure of the Speckled Band," "The Adventure of the Blanched Soldier" and "The Adventure of the Retired Colourman."

For my second pastiche, I selected "The Adventure of the Red Circle," first published in *The Strand Magazine*'s March and April 1911 issues and collected later the same year in *His Last Bow: Some Reminiscences of Sherlock Holmes,* the fourth and next-to-last volume of Holmes stories. My "The Adventure of the Red Circles," which is the most dependent of my five pastiches on a familiarity with the EQ canon, appeared in the January/February 2020 *EQMM*.

My third and fourth efforts turned "The Adventure of the Blue Carbuncle" and "The Five Orange Pips" into "The Adventure of the Black-and-Blue Carbuncle" (which is a close cousin to EQ's "The Three Students") and "The Five Orange Pipes" (which was probably the one I had the most fun writing); they appeared in the November/December 2020 and January/February 2021 issues of *EQMM*, respectively.

(In early September of 2020, I got an email from Janet, who'd just been cautioned by the magazine's long-time proofreader that the puzzle element in "The Five Orange Pipes" was very similar to an old Spencer Tracy and Katharine Hepburn movie that Janet herself hadn't seen. As it happens, I *own* that movie on DVD—I'm not mentioning its title here, in order to avoid a spoiler—and I've watched it several times and didn't recall any parallel between the film and my story. At Janet's request, though, I went back and took another look—and, sure enough, there was my puzzle! It shows up in a brief dialogue sequence between Tracy and Hepburn and has absolutely nothing whatsoever to do with the plot of the film—and in fact I think screenwriters Phoebe and Henry Ephron took it from the same old children's game that inspired my story—but, still, a reader with a taste for old movies might think "The Five Orange Pipes" plagiarizes the film. I suggested *acknowledging* the connection within my story, and Janet liked that idea. So I added about a hundred words, which resolved what might otherwise have been a problem. The story was already typeset, though, and there wasn't *room* for a hundred additional words. So Janet herself did some tinkering, taking out a couple of my sentences to make way for a reference to the movie.)

Because I was determined not to write more about the Puzzle Club than Dannay and Lee did, I felt that I had to do something in the fifth story to make it clear that there would never be—*could* never be—another one. Killing off Ellery was unthinkable; even if I'd wanted to (which I most certainly didn't), I'm sure the Dannay and Lee estates would not have permitted such a sacrilege. We'll see how you feel about the resolution I came up with. For a title, I decided to break the color pattern, since there was an obvious and really inescapable Sherlockian title crying out to be used.

In fact, there were *two* of them. Arthur Conan Doyle actually *did* kill Sherlock Holmes in an 1893 story titled "The Final Problem," so a logical title for me to use would have been "The Final Puzzle." After leaving Holmes drowned in Meiringen's Reichenbach Falls for a decade, though, Conan Doyle ultimately bowed to public pressure and, after reporting at novel length on a pre-plunge case (*The Hound of the Baskervilles*, 1902), revealed that Sherlock was not dead yet, after all, in "The Adventure of the Empty House" (1903)—and I didn't want to hint at the possibility that the adventures of the Puzzle Club were not truly at their end.

Instead, I went with Option B: in 1917, before taking another multi-year break from Holmes and Watson, Conan Doyle published a story titled "His Last Bow"—and I ultimately decided to call my Puzzle Club's fifth and final story "Their Last Bow." It was published, bringing my miniseries to a close, in the January/February 2022 issue of *EQMM*.

The idea of combining the original five Puzzle Club stories—which have never previously been collected in a single volume—with *my* five came to me early on, and again the Dannay and Lee heirs were amenable.

Partly because the stories are all rather short and partly because it just seemed like a fun thing to do, I decided to ask ten leading authorities on the EQniverse—each of whom I'm proud to call a friend—to contribute heads to the tales you'll find in these pages. They all graciously agreed, so the original five are introduced by Francis M. Nevins (author of the definitive EQ biography, *Royal Bloodline*, and one of the finest EQ pastiches, "Open Letter to Survivors"); Martin Edwards (British novelist, anthologist, and author of *The Golden Age of Murder*); Jeffrey Marks (publisher of Crippen & Landru and author of a forthcoming EQ biography); Richard Dannay (one of Frederic Dannay's sons); and Joseph Goodrich (author of the stage adaptation of *Calamity Town* and editor of *Blood Relations: Selected Letters of Ellery Queen, 1947-1950*), while my five are introduced by Janet Hutchings (*EQMM*'s longtime editor); Arthur Vidro (publisher and editor of *[Give Me That] Old Time Detection* and author of two EQ tribute stories); Kurt Sercu (founder and proprietor of *Ellery Queen: A Website on Deduction*); Jon L. Breen (author of numerous EQ pastiches and parodies); and Dale C. Andrews (author of four acclaimed EQ pastiches and co-editor of *The Misadventures of Ellery Queen* and *The Further Misadventures of Ellery Queen*). I'm grateful to all ten of them for their contributions.

Avid EQ fans may wonder about the absence of a "Challenge to the Reader" from the first two stories in this volume. This is not an accidental omission. The stories in question were originally written and published without that familiar EQ trope. When I was preparing this book, I inserted a "Challenge" at what seemed to me the appropriate moment in each of these stories, but Richard Dannay asked me to take them back out, since they weren't part of the original manuscripts. So those first two stories are presented here as written, "Challenge"-less, yet challenging to the reader nonetheless.

Once I put the Puzzle Club material and the individual story introductions together, the total length of the resulting collection was only about thirty thousand words—and Crippen & Landru publisher Jeff Marks felt that this book really ought to be longer than that.

But what else would it make sense to include—not just to make this a *bigger* book but to make it, hopefully, an even *better* one?

After batting a number of ideas back and forth, Jeff and I finally agreed that the best solution would be to include my four stories about Tyson County's Griffen family. As mentioned above, this volume marks the first time the five original Puzzle Club stories have ever appeared together—and, similarly, my EQ-inspired Griffen stories have never before been collected in a single volume.

In 1967, at the age of fifteen, I rewrote the ending of Richard Deming's "Open File," a police procedural I'd read in *EQMM*, and sent my revision off to the magazine's editorial offices in New York. I don't think I really expected to receive any kind of a response, but a couple of weeks later a two-page handwritten letter from Frederic Dannay showed up in our Long Island mailbox. After commenting favorably on what I'd sent him, he concluded: "Have you ever considered writing a detective story yourself? Seems to me, Josh—if I may—you should."

Well, of course I *did*, and the result, "E.Q. Griffen Earns His

Name," appeared in the December 1968 issue of the magazine, the three hundred and twenty-fifth entry in *EQMM*'s "Department of First Stories."

A year and a half later, E.Q. Griffen returned, in a story inevitably titled "E.Q. Griffen's Second Case," and a year after that my third published story, "Sam Buried Caesar," featured the youngest member of the Griffen family, Nero Wolfe Griffen, with Ellery not even mentioned in passing.

In 2018, I wrote a story called "50" to celebrate my fiftieth anniversary in print. It features a grown-up E.Q. Griffen, who is reminded of a murder case from fifty years ago and discovers its true solution from the comfort of his computer chair. This fourth Griffen story was published in the November/December 2018 issue of *EQMM*, and subsequently finished second in the balloting for the magazine's annual Readers Award.

These four stories—written by me but inspired by Ellery Queen (and Rex Stout)—seem to Jeff and me to be an appropriate coda for this "collaborative" collection, and in the same spirit which led me to invite ten noted EQologists to introduce the ten Puzzle Club stories, we've decided to reprint not just the Griffen stories themselves but also their original *EQMM* introductions, the first three of which were written by Fred Dannay and the fourth by Janet Hutchings. We hope you'll agree that these stories add another layer of interest to the book you now hold in your hands.

All that said, I've kept you waiting long enough. Without further ado, I welcome you to the ten adventures of the Puzzle Club, first Ellery Queen's version and then mine, followed by the four Griffen-family stories. Enjoy!

Josh Pachter
Midlothian, Virginia
May 2022

PART I

THE ORIGINALS
by Ellery Queen

THE LITTLE SPY

originally published in *Cavalier* (January 1965)

INTRODUCTION BY FRANCIS M. NEVINS:

To appreciate the first five stories in this book, you have to be aware of two fundamental facts:

First, the division of labor between the first cousins who wrote about and under the byline of Ellery Queen was that Frederic Dannay (1905–1982) created the detailed skeletons, in the form of a twenty-thousand- to twenty-five-thousand-word plot synopsis for each novel, and Manfred B. Lee (1905–1971) put the flesh onto those bones.

Second, the Puzzle Club stories were written during the period in the 1960s when Manny was suffering from writer's block and unable to collaborate with Fred.

"The Little Spy" was the first of five Queen stories revolving around a tiny coterie of enthusiasts who met regularly to propound riddles to each other. The concept was probably Fred's alone, but in effect the series was a fictionalization of the cousins' 1939 radio show Author! Author!—itself, as Josh Pachter points out in his introduction to this volume, perhaps influenced by Agatha Christie's Tuesday Club—in which Fred and Manny and two guests challenged themselves to devise ad lib a rationale for the bizarre situation dramatized at the start of each program. In the Puzzle Club stories, the challenge is to construct not a beginning but a resolution.

Fred and Manny collaborated by combat. Manny's main interests were character, atmosphere and social realism, while Fred's were more abstract and cerebral. I see Manny's spiritual kin as the character Joel McCrea played in the Preston Sturges movie Sullivan's Travels (1941), a Hollywood director who hates the hit comedies he's helmed and burns to create a Steinbeck-like "social consciousness" epic with the title O Brother, Where Art Thou? Fred, on the other hand, I see as spiritual kin to the great Argentinian author Jorge Luis Borges (1899–1986), who was a Queen fan (almost certainly on Fred's side of the equation rather than Manny's) and some of whose best known stories, like "The Garden of Forking Paths" and "Death and the Compass," are set in Cloud Cuckoo Lands similar to the kind that delighted Fred and infuriated Manny. The cousins' correspondence is full of passages in which they snipe at each other. "He gives me the most ridiculous plots to work with," Manny told his son Rand after a heated phone conversation with Fred, "and expects me to make them realistic."

In "The Little Spy" and the other Puzzle Club stories completed in Fred's lifetime, Manny's contribution if any is all but invisible. These tales are pure riddles. Insist upon the characterization and atmosphere and vivid prose contributed by Manny to the finest Queen novels and stories, and you're bound to be disappointed. Take them as unadulterated specimens of late Fred Dannay, though, and you're much more likely to appreciate the first five stories in this book.

The letter was written in a secretive hand on paper as thick as a pharaoh's papyrus. Instead of a name or a crest, its engraved monogram consisted of one large gold ticklesome question mark.

"My dear Mr. Queen," Ellery read. "It is the pleasure of the Puzzle Club to invite you to our next regular meeting, which takes place at 7:30 P.M. Wednesday at the address below. Purpose: to offer you our membership test, which we believe without modesty will challenge your logical powers. Ours is a very small, congenial group. There are no dues or other obligations. You will be the only outsider present. Informal dress. We hope you will respond affirmatively."

None of Ellery's reference books, including the telephone directory, listed a Puzzle Club. On the other hand, the signature and address made it unlikely that this was the gambit to a mugging party or badger game. So Ellery dashed off an acceptance note, and Wednesday evening found him, at seven-thirty to the tick, pushing the bell of a penthouse foyer in the nobbiest reaches of Park Avenue.

The lordly Englishman who opened the door turned out to be a butler, who took his hat and vanished, and the rumpled-looking Texan giant who greeted him was unmistakably Ellery's correspondent and host. The big man's name was Syres, and he was one of the ten wealthiest men in the United States.

"On the dot," Syres boomed. "Welcome, Mr. Queen!" He was all but grinding his muscular hands, and he rushed Ellery into a museum of massive Western furniture, studded leather, burnished woods, antique carpets, Old Masters, and twinkling crystal and copper. "I see you're admiring my traditionalism. I loathe contemporary anything."

Except, Ellery thought, *contemporary oil wells and the profits therefrom,* but he meekly followed his host into a living room vast enough for a hidalgo's rancho.

In a moment Ellery was shaking hands with the other members of the Puzzle Club. Three were present besides Syres, and not altogether to his surprise Ellery recognized each of them. The dark, tall, mustache-eyebrowed man was the celebrated criminal lawyer Darnell, who was being mentioned frequently these days for the next opening on the Supreme Court. The trim, short, peach-cheeked one was the noted psychiatrist Dr. Vreeland. The third was Emmy Wandermere, the poet, a wisp of a woman with shocking blue eyes and the handclasp of a man.

Ellery gathered that the Puzzle Club was of recent origin. It had no more purpose than any other association in gamesmanship, perhaps less, and while its members were all prominently implicated in the world as it was, the Club's bylaws, he was promptly told, forbade discussion at its monthly meetings of any subject not connected with puzzles.

As the psychiatric Dr. Vreeland put it, "Other people meet regularly to play bridge. We meet to mystify each other—as man has done with riddles since prehistory—in a sort of ritual adoration of the question mark."

They sat him down in a roomy armchair near the man-high fireplace, and the English butler brought him a Scotch, a napkin, and a little tray of sizzling canapés.

"And that's all you get, Mr. Queen, until the test is over," the oilman explained. "We don't eat dinner until afterward."

"The Arabs have a proverb," said Dr. Vreeland. "When the stomach speaks, wisdom is silent."

"Or as Stevenson put it," murmured Miss Wandermere, "the sort who eat unduly must never hope for glory."

"You see, Queen, we want you to be at your best," said Darnell, the lawyer, staring piercingly at their victim. "Our membership rules are quite harsh. For example, application is by unanimous invitation only. Our fifth member, Dr. Arkavy, the Nobel Prize-winning biochemist, who's away at a science conference, voted by cable all the way from Moscow to invite you."

"You should understand, too," said tycoon Syres, "that if you fail to solve the puzzle we're going to throw at you tonight, you'll never be invited to try again."

"Harsh, indeed," said Ellery, nodding. "You titillate me. How exactly is the puzzle propounded?"

"In story form," said the lady poet. "How else?"

"Have I the option of asking questions?"

"As many as you like," said the little psychiatrist.

"In that case," Ellery said, "you-all may fire when ready."

"It happened during World War Two," the multimillionaire host began the story. "You'll remember how hectic everything was—government departments mushrooming overnight, new bureaus scrambling to get organized, all sorts of people pulled out of the woodwork to help with the war effort, and security officers going crazy with the work load suddenly dumped on their shoulders."

"In a certain very important government war bureau newly set up," psychiatrist Vreeland said as he lit a cigar, "one of the working force taken on was a little man named Tarleton—J. Aubrey Tarleton—who came out of retirement to do his bit for Uncle Sam. J. Aubrey was an ex-civil servant with a good if undistinguished record in government service. The bureau was an essential and very sensitive one. There was no time to do more than a conventional security check, but Tarleton's long record seemed to speak for itself."

"If you had seen old Mr. Tarleton," Miss Wandermere, the poet, took up the tale, "he would have struck you as a throwback—

say, someone out of the British civil service in Rudyard Kipling's day. He had a Colonel Blimp mustache, he invariably dressed in ultraconservative clothes of Edwardian cut, he actually wore a piped vest and spats, carried a silver-headed cane, and he was never without a boutonnière pinned to his lapel, usually a white gardenia. A spic-and-span, courtly little old gentleman out of a long-dead age.

"His tastes were as elegantly old-fashioned," the lady poet went on, "as his manners. For instance, Mr. Tarleton was something of a gourmet and a connoisseur of vintages. Also, he would talk endlessly about his hobby, which was painting tiny landscapes on little ovals of ivory and ceramic—even worse, going on and on about his collection of eighteenth century miniatures by Richard Cosway and Ozias Humphry and other artists practically no one had ever heard of. In short, he was a good deal of a bore, and the younger people in the bureau especially vied with one another inventing new ways of avoiding him."

"Then something happened," lawyer Darnell chimed in, "that threw the spotlight on little Mr. Tarleton. It was shortly before D-Day, and the dapper old gent suddenly wangled a priority airline passage to London. Just then, Intelligence received an anonymous tip that Tarleton was in the pay of the Nazis, that he was a German spy. There were thousands of such tips during the war, most of them checking out as baseless— the result of malice, or spy fever, or what-have-you. But in view of Tarleton's access to top-secret material, and rather than take a chance at such a critical time, they yanked old Tarleton off the plane just as it was about to take off, and they gave him a going-over."

"This," asserted oilman Syres gravely, "was the most thorough search in the long and honorable history of spy-catching. It took a very long time, because at first it was entirely unsuccessful. In the end, of course, they found it."

"The plans for the Allied invasion of Europe, no doubt," Ellery said, smiling.

"Exactly," said Miss Wandermere, looking faintly disapproving. "The date cycle for D-Day, the location of the landings, the strength of the Allied forces—everything the German high command needed to smash the invasion in its tracks. There it was, to the last detail, all written down in plain uncoded English. The question you've got to answer, Mr. Queen, is a simple one. But watch out! Where did the Intelligence people find the spy message?"

"Or to put it the other way," Darnell, the criminal lawyer, said, "where did Tarleton conceal the spy message?"

"May I rule out the plane?" Ellery asked promptly. "That is, he didn't conceal it somewhere on board just before he was grabbed? Or in his luggage, or someone else's luggage?"

"He did not."

"He didn't pass it to a confederate?"

"No."

"The message was found on his person?"

"It was."

"Well, let's see." Ellery frowned. "I assume the obvious places of possible concealment yielded nothing: hat, coat, vest, trousers, shirt, tie, shoes, socks, spats, underclothing, galoshes or rubbers, that sort of thing?"

There was a general nod.

"The flower in his buttonhole? It was a real flower?"

"Nature's own," said Dr. Vreeland.

"The contents of his pockets?"

"Every object he carried in his pockets was minutely gone over, without result."

"The pockets themselves?"

"Concealed nothing."

"A *secret* pocket? Anywhere in his clothing?"

"No."

"Was he carrying a book?"

"No."

"A newspaper? Magazine? Directory? Any printed material whatever?"

"None."

"There must have been some printed matter in his wallet: credit cards, driver's license—"

"All carefully examined for secret writing," Syres chuckled. "Including, I might add, the material of the wallet itself. And no dice."

"Was his bare skin examined for secret writing?"

"It was, including his scalp, ears, and finger- and toenails," the oilman grinned, "and there wasn't any. They looked under infrared and ultraviolet and every other kind of light known to science. They peered at every square inch through a microscope. They used every chemical known to bring out secret writing. They even parboiled him—applied heat."

"Thorough," said Ellery dryly. "Well." He reflected. "Was he tattooed with some design that looked innocuous but actually concealed a hidden message?"

"In the naked state," Miss Wandermere assured him, "old Mr. Tarleton was as pinkly unmarred as a healthy six-month fetus."

"And I take it the usual fluoroscope and X-ray examintions were made without turning the message up in the old spy's intrior?"

"You take it correctly, Mr. Queen."

"His mustache!" Ellery said. "Under it."

"Ingenious mind, this fellow," lawyer Darnell said admiringly. "You mean Tarleton wrote the message on his upper lip and then grew a mustache over it? Well, Intelligence thought of that. They shaved off his mustache and found nothing underneath but lip."

"Interesting." Ellery was pulling on his nose, a sure sign of deep cerebration. "Let's tackle objects that might conceal the message. Stop me if I hit one that's relevant. Watch, wrist or pocket type? Ring? Hearing aid? Hairpiece? Glass eye? Contact lenses? The shafts of eyeglasses? False teeth? False finger or toe? Any prosthetic device at all?"

"Heavens, you'll have the old traitor made up of bits and pieces, Mr. Queen," laughed the lady poet. "No to all your sugestions."

"Key-ring? Card case? Cufflinks? Tie clasp? Belt? Suspenders? Pipe? Tobacco pouch? Cigarettes? Cigarette case? Snuffbox? Pillbox?"

Ellery went on and on until he ran out of ideas. To each suggestion, they shook their heads.

There was silence. The members of the Puzzle Club glanced at one another significantly.

"Buttons," Ellery said, of a sudden. "Hollowed-out buttons! No? Ah, I've forgotten something!"

"What's that?" asked Darnell curiously.

"His silver-headed cane!"

But they all shook their heads, smiling. And there was silence again.

"Well, I've eliminated everything you've told me about the old boy, and lots more. Or have I?"

"To that question, Mr. Queen," said Syres, smiling even more broadly, "you'll have to provide your own answer. Fascinating problem, isn't it?"

"And damned smart Intelligence people," Ellery mourned. "Final question: what if there's more than one answer, and I hit one you haven't thought of?"

There was incredulous hilarity.

"In that case," the lady poet said, "we'd probably elect you president of the club."

"Now, Mr. Queen," said Syres, "you may retire to my study to think, or take a walk down Park Avenue, or spend your time any way you please while chewing on the puzzle. Unfortunately, we can't let you have more than an hour. My chef Charlot's dinner won't be edible after nine o'clock. Which is your pleasure?"

"Inasmuch as all this ratiocination has made me hungry," Ellery said, grinning back, "I think I'll answer your puzzle right now.

"The clue," Ellery chuckled in the attentive silence, "stemmed from old Tarleton's hobby—his painting of miniatures. It naturally suggested that he had written the spy message in miniature—in lettering so small it could be read only through a strong magnifying glass. That much was obvious.

"The question, of course, was: on which object Tarleton carried on his person was the miniaturized spy message inscribed?

"I just questioned whether I had covered everything about the old spy that you people had mentioned in your description of him. Of course I had not. I eliminated every possible object on Tarleton's person but one. The message must therefore have been written in miniature on that one object.

"Old Tarleton was in the tradition of the very select few who have been able to inscribe the Gettysburg Address or the Lord's Prayer on an object no bigger than an oversized period.

"He wrote the spy message on the head of the pin that secured the flower to his lapel."

"Miss Wandermere and gentlemen," said the tycoon heartily, "I give you the newest member of the Puzzle Club!"

THE PRESIDENT REGRETS

originally published in *Diners Club Magazine* (September 1965)

INTRODUCTION BY JEFFREY MARKS:

Early in the twentieth century, a number of American presidents were fans of crime fiction. Teddy Roosevelt read Poe and Mary Roberts Rinehart. After Woodrow Wilson's stroke, his second wife read mysteries to him to pass the time. Calvin Coolidge enjoyed the novels of S.S. Van Dine. And Herbert Hoover read voraciously in the mystery field.

Franklin Delano Roosevelt actually had an idea for a mystery: how, he wondered, would a man disappear with millions of dollars? This prompt was presented to Fulton Oursler, who was the editor of Liberty *magazine (and is better remembered by mystery readers for the books and stories he wrote as Anthony Abbot), and a group of mystery writers collectively wrote the novel, which was serialized a chapter at a time in the pages of* Liberty. *Though the book was not well written and lacked a cohesive ending, it appeared briefly on the best-sellers list as* The President's Mystery Story *and was eventually turned into a movie. (Decades later, Erle Stanley Gardner came up with a viable solution, and a 1967 reprint of the book was retitled* The President's Mystery Plot.*)*

In the current century, mystery readers have seen a number of books with US presidents as co-authors and/or characters: James Patterson and Bill Clinton have teamed up for two thrillers set within America's executive branch, and Barack Obama and Joe Biden are the main characters in two crime novels by Andrew Shaffer.

All of which brings us to Ellery Queen, and the fact that EQ the author wrote several short stories in which EQ the character solved mysteries involving an American president.

In "The President's Half Disme"—a recycled radio play which first appeared in 1947 and was anthologized in Calendar of Crime*—the* *reader is informed that George Washington once planted a grove of trees and buried items of significance, including a "half disme" (or "half dime"), beneath one of them. When the original landowner's poverty-stricken descendants need to find this long-lost treasure, Ellery comes to the rescue.*

Abraham Lincoln was so entranced with Edgar Allan Poe that he could quote entire sections of Poe's stories, such as "The Gold-Bug." In "Abraham Lincoln's Clue," which appeared in 1965, we learn that Lincoln and Poe both signed the same copy of a book, making it a unique historical memento. Lincoln devised an uncanny way of hiding the book according to methods laid down by Poe—and, a century later, Ellery again steps in to unravel a president's reasoning.

And then came "The President Regrets." The second of Queen's Puzzle Club stories, it cleverly revolves around the idea of the U.S. president as a mystery aficionado. Although the titular president is not mentioned by name, the story was published in Diners Club Magazine *in September of 1965, which implies that the president in question must have been Lyndon Johnson. By all accounts, unfortunately, LBJ was not a mystery buff—which perhaps explains why the president regretfully finds a reason to decline the invitation to attend a meeting of the Puzzle Club.*

The Puzzle Club is a congeries of very important people drawn together by unimportant purpose but common passion—to wit: to mystify one another. Their pleasure, in short, is puzzles.

Application is by invitation only, and membership must be won, the applicant having to submit to an Ordeal by Puzzle. If he survives the test, it earns him automatic admission.

Shortly after Ellery became the Puzzle Club's sixth regular member, it was proposed and unanimously voted to invite the President of the United States to apply for membership.

This was no frivolous motion; the members took their puzzles seriously, and the president was known to be a devotee of mysteries in all lawful forms. Besides, the club's founder and first member, multimillionaire oilman Syres, had been buddy-buddy with the occupant of the White House since their youthful days as riggers in the Texas oilfields.

The invitation went to Washington, and rather to Ellery's surprise the president promptly accepted the challenge. In deference to affairs of state, he was urged to designate his own date, which he did, but when Ellery arrived at Syres' Park Avenue penthouse on the appointed evening to find the membership assembled, he was greeted with gloomy news. The president regretted that he could not make it, after all. A Secret Service man, just departed, had brought the message that a new crisis in the Middle East had caused a last-minute cancellation of the president's flight to New York.

"What shall we do now?" asked Darnell, the famous criminal lawyer.

"There's no point in wasting the puzzle we've prepared for the president," said Dr. Vreeland, the well-known psychiatrist. "Let's save it for whenever he can get here."

"It's too bad Dr. Arkavy is still attending that symposium in Moscow," said wispy little Emmy Wandermere, the poet. Dr. Arkavy was a Nobel Prize-winning biochemist. "He has such a fertile mind, he can always come up with something on the spur of the moment."

"Maybe our newest member can help us out," said their Texan host. "What do you say, Queen? You must have a hundred problems at your fingers' ends, from your long experience as a writer and a detective."

"Let me think." Ellery cogitated. Then he chuckled. "All right. Give me a few minutes to work out the details."

It took him far less.

"I'm ready," he said. "I suggest we engage in some collective improvisation to begin with. Since this is going to be a murder mystery, we will obviously require a victim. Any suggestions?"

"A woman, of course," the lady poet said at once.

"Reeking of glamour," said the psychiatrist.

"That," said the criminal lawyer, "would seem to call for a Hollywood movie star."

"Good enough," Ellery said. "And a glamour girl of the screen calls for a glamorous name. Let's call her ... oh, Valetta Van Buren. Agreed?"

"Valetta Van Buren." Miss Wandermere considered the suggestion. "Yes. She personifies sex in her roles—a smoky witch with enormous cold full-moon eyes. Does that follow, Mr. Queen?"

"Perfectly. Well," Ellery went on, "Valetta is in New York to attend the première of her latest picture and to do the circuit of TV appearances in promotion of it. But this hasn't proved an ordinary publicity tour. In fact, Valetta has had a frightening experience. It so shook her up that she wrote me an agitated letter about it, which, by the magic of coincidence, I received just this morning."

"*In* which," Dr. Vreeland pressed, "she said—"

"—that during this New York visit she permitted herself to be squired about town by four men—"

"—who are all, naturally, in love with her?" asked the lady poet.

"You guessed it, Miss Wandermere. She identified the four in her letter. One is that notorious man-about-town and playboy John Thrushbottom Taylor the Third—and if you haven't heard of Mr. Taylor, it's because I just made him up. The second is that wolf—in both senses—of Wall Street named ... well, let's call him A. Palmer Harrison. The third, of course, is the latest rage among society Pop Art painters, Leonardo Price. And the last of the quartet is—let's see—Biff Wilson, the professional football player."

"A likely story," grinned oilman Syres.

Ellery made a professional bridge of his fingers. "Now, having named the four men for me, Valetta went on to say that all four proposed marriage to her—each of them on the same day, yesterday. Unhappily, our ineffable Valetta felt nothing for any of them—nothing permanent, at any rate. She rejected all four. It was a busy day for Miss Van Buren, and she would have enjoyed it, except for one thing."

"One of them," said the criminal lawyer, "turned ugly."

"Exactly, Darnell. Valetta wrote me that three of them took their turndowns with approximations of grace. But the fourth flew into a homicidal rage and threatened to kill her. She was terrified he would try to carry out his threat and asked me to get in touch with her at once. She felt reluctant to go to the police, she wrote, because of the bad publicity it would bring her."

"What happened then?" asked Syres.

"I phoned, of course," Ellery replied, "as soon as I finished reading her letter. But—would you believe it?—I was too late. She was murdered last night, a short time after she must have mailed the letter. So the screen has lost its sexiest pot, and millions of red-blooded Americans at this very moment are mourning the sheer waste of it all."

"How," asked Darnell, "was the foul deed done?"

"I could tell you," Ellery said, "that she was done in by a Tasmanian yo-yo, but I won't be unfair: the nature of the weapon is irrelevant. I will say this, however, to avoid complications: Valetta *was* murdered by the suitor who threatened her life."

"And is that all?" asked the tycoon.

"No, I've saved the kicker for last, Mr. Syres. Valetta's letter gave me one clue. In writing about the four men, she said she'd noticed she had something in common with three of the four, and that the fourth was the one who had threatened her."

"Ah," said Dr. Vreeland. "Then all we have to establish is the nature of the common denominator. The three sharing it with Valetta would be innocent. By elimination, therefore, the one left over has to be the guilty man."

Ellery nodded. "And now—if my initiation at our last meeting was a criterion—the floor is open for questions."

"I take it," the lady poet murmured, "that we may disregard the obvious possibilities of connection—that Valetta and three of the men were of the same age, or had the same color hair, or the same religious affiliation, or came from the same town or state, or attended the same college, or were investors or board members in the same corporation—that sort of thing?"

Ellery laughed. "Yes, you may disregard those."

"Social position?" the multimillionaire ventured. "Three of the men you described—playboy John Something Taylor, Wall Street man A. Palmer Harrison, Pop Art painter Price—did they all come from high society? That probably wouldn't be true of the pro football player, What's-His-Name."

"It just so happens," Ellery mourned, "that Pop Art painter Price was born in a Greenwich Village pad. And Valetta, of course, hailed from the slums of Chicago."

They pondered.

"Had three of the four men ever served with Valetta," asked Darnell suddenly, "on the same jury?"

"No."

"On a TV panel show?" asked the poet quickly.

"No, Miss Wandermere."

"Don't tell me," said Dr. Vreeland, smiling, "that Valetta Van Buren and three of her suitors at one juncture in their lives shared the same psychiatrist's couch?"

"That's a good solution, Doctor. But it's not the solution I have in mind."

"Politics," the oilman said. "Valetta and three of the suitors are registered in the same party."

"My information, Mr. Syres," said Ellery, "is that Valetta was an incorrigible Democrat, the playboy and the Wall Street man are conservative Republicans, and Price and Biff Wilson have never voted in their lives."

Miss Wandermere suddenly said, "It isn't anything like that. Am I right, Mr. Queen, in assuming that all the relevant facts were given to us in the body of your story?"

"I wondered if someone was going to ask that," Ellery chuckled. "That's exactly so, Miss Wandermere. There's really no need to ask questions at all."

"Then I for one need more time," said the tycoon. "What about the rest of you?"

At their abstracted nods, their host rose.

"I suggest we make an exception tonight and eat Charlot's exquisite dinner before we crack Queen's puzzle."

Miss Wandermere's shocking blue eyes sparkled with enlightenment during Charlot's *mousseline de saumon*. Darnell's mustache-sized brows lifted with elation over the *suprêmes de volaille aux huîtres*. Dr. Vreeland uttered his self-congratulatory exclamation at the serving of the *selle de veau à l'Orientale*. And their host, Syres, achieved sweet victory over his *Charlotte Chantilly*. But no one uttered a word until they were seated about the drawing room again over espresso and brandy.

"I detect from this and that," Ellery said, "that none of you encountered any real difficulty with my little puzzle."

"It's too bad the president had to miss this," Syres roared. "It was made to order, Queen, for his type of mind! Are you all quite ready?"

There was a universal nod.

"In that case," Ellery said, with resignation, "which of Valetta's four swains murdered her?"

"Females first, always," said Dr. Vreeland, with a gallant nod to Miss Wandermere.

"The key to the answer," said the lady poet promptly, "consists of the fact, Mr. Queen, that you really told us just one thing about Valetta and her four suitors. It follows that whatever she and three of the four men had in common must relate to that thing."

"A logic I can't dispute," murmured Ellery. "And that thing was?"

Darnell grinned. "What the anticipation of the president's visit here tonight suggested to you when we asked for an impromptu puzzle: their *names*."

"You named the movie star Valetta Van Buren," said Syres. "Van Buren—the name of a President of the United States."

"Then playboy John Thrushbottom Taylor the Third," said the psychiatrist. "You buried that one, Queen! But of course Taylor is the name of a President of the United States, too—Zachary Taylor."

"And the Wall Street man, A. Palmer Harrison," the lawyer said. "Harrison, William Henry. Also Harrison, Benjamin."

"And professional football player Biff Wilson," Miss Wandermere twinkled. "That 'Biff' was masterly, Mr. Queen. But of course Wilson, for Woodrow Wilson."

"Which leaves only *one* character whose name," said the oilman, "bears *no* cross-reference to a president's name—Leonardo Price. So Price, the Pop Art painter, murdered Valetta. You almost had me fooled, Queen. Taylor, Van Buren, Harrison! That was tricky, picking the more obscure presidents."

"You could hardly expect me to name one of my characters Eisenhower," Ellery grinned. "Which reminds me"—he raised his brandy snifter—"here's to our absent president ... and may he turn out to be the next member of the Puzzle Club!"

THE THREE STUDENTS

originally published in *Playboy* (March 1971)

INTRODUCTION BY MARTIN EDWARDS:

"The Three Students" was the first of three Puzzle Club mysteries that appeared in quick succession in 1971, as Ellery Queen's remarkable career was drawing to a close.

At this distance of time, it seems extraordinary that this story and "The Odd Man" were first published in Playboy. *Ellery Queen was, after all, a cerebral detective whose career prompted Dashiell Hammett's cheeky question: "Mr. Queen, what can you tell us about your famous character's sex life, if any?" In the Queen stories, as Joseph Goodrich put it in a piece he wrote for Kurt Sercu's EQ website, "the emphasis is on deduction, not seduction."*

However, perhaps on reflection the appearance of Ellery Queen in Playboy *is not quite such a surprise. Throughout their career, the cousins who wrote as Queen showed great commercial acumen, and the magazine did pay well and guarantee an extensive readership. No doubt as a concession to the market, this story includes passing reference to a "sex mad" student and also a topless exotic dancer.*

Overall, "The Three Students" fits the pattern established when the Puzzle Club series began in 1965: the solution to the mystery can be deduced from a clue in the text. In this story, the clue will only be understood by a reader who possesses a specialized piece of knowledge. In other words, although it is a fair-play story, it is fair play more akin to that practiced by R. Austin Freeman, many of whose puzzles are solved thanks to obscure snippets of scientific expertise, rather than in the Agatha Christie vein; her clues could usually be interpreted by alert readers without the use of special know-how.

Detective fiction featuring clubs of puzzle enthusiasts with a penchant for solving mysteries dates back more than ninety years. As is noted in Josh Pachter's general introduction to this volume, the pleasing concept of the Puzzle Club calls to mind Christie's Tuesday Night Club—but also Anthony Berkeley's Crimes Circle, whose detective work forms the heart of his masterpiece, The Poisoned Chocolates Case. *The appeal of the concept endures to this day and is at least as strong as ever. For proof of this, one need look no further than at two recent and very popular British novels, Richard Osman's best-seller* The Thursday Murder Club *and Robert Thorogood's* The Marlow Murder Club ... *as well as Josh's enjoyable revival of the Puzzle Club, more than half a century after its creation.*

The membership of the Puzzle Club numbered six—one of whom, Arkavy, the Nobel biochemist, was almost never free to attend a meeting—making it, as far as Ellery knew, the world's most exclusive society.

Its only agenda was to solve mysteries made up by the members and then, regardless of outcome, to slaver, sample, and gorge at the feast prepared by the master chef of their host and the founder of the Club, Syres, the oil multimillionaire. Members took turns playing problem solver, and this evening the rotation had come round to Ellery again.

Having been duly installed in the "Problem Chair" in Syres's wide-open-spaces-style penthouse salon, Ellery tilted the bottle at his elbow and then settled back with his glass to face the music and its composers.

Little Emmy Wandermere, the Pulitzer Prize-winning poet, had been designated to conduct the overture. "The scene is the office of the president of a small college," she began, "the office being situated on the ground floor of the Administration Building. President Xavier—"

"X," Ellery said instantly. "Significant?"

"You're a quick starter," the poetess said. "In this discipline, Mr. Queen, significance lies in the ear of the listener. I should like to go on. President Xavier has one child, a grown son—"

"Who is, of course, a student at the college."

"Who happens to be nothing of the sort. The son is a high-school dropout immersed in the study of yoga and Zen."

"His name?"

"Ah, his name. All right, Mr. Queen, having consulted my instant muse, she tells me that the son was christened Xenophon, President Xavier having taken his doctorate in Greek history. Now Xenophon Xavier has just become engaged to be married—"

"*To* a student?"

"You seem to have students on the brain. Not to a student, no. She's a topless exotic dancer Xenophon met through his guru. May I suggest that you listen, Mr. Queen? The boy's father—and if you want to know President Xavier's Christian name, too, by the way, it's St. Francis—has undertaken to provide the engagement ring. He's just come from visiting his safe-deposit box, in fact. The first thing President Xavier does on entering his office is to place the ring on his desk. It's a very valuable ring, of course, a family heirloom."

"Is there any other kind?" Ellery asked mercilessly. "Whereupon"—and he paused to sip his Scotch—"enter Suspects."

Syres nodded. "A delegation of three students who represent three dissident groups at the college."

"One," said Darnell, the lawyer, "a law student named Adams."

"Two," said Vreeland, the psychiatrist, "a medical student named Barnes."

"And three," said poet Wandermere, "a literature major named Carver."

"Adams, Barnes, Carver," Ellery said. "A, B, C. We're certainly relying on the basics tonight. But proceed."

"Adams, the law student, demands that the football team's star pass receiver, who's been expelled from the school after a secret hearing," said lawyer Darnell, "be reinstated on the grounds that he was the victim of a Star Chamber proceeding and had been denied due process."

"The college expelled its star receiver?" Ellery shook his head. "This is obviously a fantasy."

"Derision, Queen, will get you nowhere," Dr. Vreeland said severely. "As for Barnes, like many med students he's sex mad, and he's there to demand that the curfew restrictions for coeds visiting the boys' dorms be lifted entirely."

"And young Carver is there," Miss Wandermere said, "to demand a separate and autonomous Black Culture Department, staffed entirely by Blacks."

"There's a lively discussion, President Xavier promises to take the three demands under advisement, and the students exit." Syres held up his saddle-like hand. "Not yet, Queen! Xavier then goes to lunch, locking the only door of his office. He's away, oh, twenty minutes—"

"A fast eater," Ellery murmured.

"When he unlocks the door on his return, he notices two things. The first—"

"—is that the ring, which with convenient forgetfulness he'd left on his desk," Ellery said promptly, "is gone."

"Yes," Darnell said, "and the second is a folded slip of paper lying on the floor near the desk."

"Which says—?"

"Which says"—and Dr. Vreeland showed his formidable teeth like a playful wolf—"in unidentifiable block lettering, naturally—are you paying attention, Queen?"

"Which says," Emmy Wandermere said, "as follows: 'On old Olympus' towering top / A Finn and German viewed a hop.' Terrible verse. I can thankfully say, Mr. Queen, I'm not responsible for it."

Ellery mumbled, "Would you mind repeating that?"

The challengers exchanged congratulatory smirks. Miss Wandermere cheerfully repeated the doggerel.

"Nonsense verse." Ellery was still mumbling. "Or—" He stopped and shook his head, like a fighter shaking off a stiff jab. "Let's hack away the underbrush first. Was the door tampered with?"

"I'll make it simple for you," Syres said in a kind voice. "Entry was by the window, which had been forced. No fingerprints. No clues."

"I take it that, during their visit to Xavier's office, Adams, Barnes, and Carver had the ring in plain view?"

"Right there on the desk," Dr. Vreeland said. "They all saw it."

"Who else knew the ring was in the office?"

"No one."

"Not even his son, Xenophon?"

"Not even his son, Xenophon."

"Or his prospective daughter-in-law?"

"That's right."

"Was the ring visible from the window?"

"It was not," said Miss Wandermere. "It was lying behind a bust of—"

"Xanthippe, I know. Was there an open transom above the door?"

"No transom at all."

"A fireplace?"

"No fireplace."

"And you wouldn't insult me by a secret passage. Well, then, the thief has to have been one of the three students. Which is the conclusion I assume you wanted me to reach."

"True," Darnell said.

"And Xavier is positive the paper with the verse wasn't on the floor when he left for lunch?"

Glances were exchanged once more. "We hadn't thought of that possibility," the oilman confessed. "No, Queen, the paper wasn't there when Xavier left the office."

"So it must have been dropped by the thief."

"Accidentally, Queen," the lawyer said. "It was later learned that the thief took a handkerchief out of his pocket to wrap around his hand—he didn't want to leave fingerprints—and, as he did so, the paper fell out of his pocket."

"He made off with the ring," the poetess said, "without noticing that he'd left the verse behind."

"So you don't have to ask any further questions," the psychiatrist said. "Tough one, Queen, isn't it? We were absolutely determined to stump you tonight. And by the superegos of Freud, Jung, and Adler, friends, I believe we've done it!"

"Give a fellow a chance, will you?" Ellery growled. "'On old Olympus' towering top / A Finn and German viewed a hop.'"

"We've got him on the run, all right," the oil king chortled. "Usual one-hour time limit, Queen. Mustn't keep old Charlot's dinner waiting. What is it?"

Emmy Wandermere: "Oh, no!"

Dr. Vreeland: "Impossible!"

Darnell, incredulously: "You've got it?"

"Well, I'll tell you," Ellery said with unruffled brow, a vision of peace. "Yes."

CHALLENGE TO THE READER

Who stole the ring? And how did Ellery know?

THE SOLUTION

"'On old Olympus' towering top / A Finn and German viewed a hop,'" Ellery said. "As verse, it's gibberish. That made me dig into my gibberish pile, which is eighty feet higher than Mount Everest. My curse is that I never forget anything, no matter how useless.

"Having recognized the nature of the verse, I knew the thief couldn't have been Adams, the law student, or the lit major—much as you tried to make Carver your red (or should I say Black?) herring.

"'On old Olympus' towering top' et cetera is a traditional mnemonic aid for remembering the names of the twelve cranial nerves. The 'o' of 'On,' for instance, stands for 'olfactory'—the olfactory nerve. The 'o' of 'old' stands for the optic nerve, and so on. The verse is used in medical schools by students. The paper therefore dropped from the pocket of Barnes, the med student, making him the thief of the ring."

"I could have sworn on my plaque of Hippocrates that you'd fall flat on your face when I suggested this one," Dr. Vreeland said glumly.

"*Queen erat demonstrandum,*" Emmy Wandermere murmured. "And now, gentlemen, shall we render unto Charlot?"

THE ODD MAN

originally published in *Playboy* (June 1971)

INTRODUCTION BY JOSEPH GOODRICH:

I am easily bamboozled, and I hate it. This is one of the reasons I've always favored the later novels of Ellery Queen, where the brain-busting aspect of the mystery is leavened with sundry moral, psychological, and religious matters. Roman hats and Greek coffins are of less interest to me than ten days' wonders and many-tailed cats.

I make an exception for the stories involving the Puzzle Club, whose members freely indulge, as Queen admirably phrased it, "in a sort of ritual adoration of the question mark." If a novel is a three-course dinner and a short story a sandwich, then the Puzzle Club stories are bonbons: literary confections easily, delightfully, and quickly consumed. Be careful not to gorge on them, however; they must be savored.

Until recently, in fact, they had *to be savored because there were so few of them. As I'm sure you know by now, Dannay and Lee only wrote five stories featuring the club, and Josh Pachter has rounded out the batch with five new stories of his own.*

If the Puzzle Club stories are not the ultimate expression of Ellery Queen, they are *the ultimate expression of Frederic Dannay's penchant for puzzle making. Campus unrest, drug dealing, Middle East crises and other late-Sixties/early-Seventies matters figure into the tales, but that's contemporaneous window dressing. There's no room for the moral and ethical matters that animate longer and more encompassing EQ works. The God-like manipulator, so often the villain of those novels, is a far more genial deity in these stories; no trace can be found of the fierce Old Testament Divinity. The stories revel in artificiality, and the fact of game-playing is accentuated—it is, indeed, the entire conceit. Dannay is free to come up with the damnedest conundrums and leave his readers—well,* this *reader, at least—pleas-*

antly and thoroughly mystified.

"The Odd Man" offers Ellery a typically clever challenge … and a unique twist. There are not one, not two, but three *possible solutions to the evening's brain-twister, two of which are provided by the stalwart Mr. Queen to the amazement and chagrin of the other club members. An astonishing feat, especially when one considers that all this is accomplished in less than three thousand words, a sign of Dannay's fecundity as a creator of clues.*

As the story notes, the puzzles propounded by the Puzzle Club are "as painstakingly planned for the battle of wits as if an empire depended on the outcome." In truth, the fate of nations does not depend on what happens in the Club's plush Park Avenue setting. The riddles are (for all their thefts and murders) friendly challenges, an invitation to join in the fun-and-games. Neither life nor death hinges on the proper answer to a puzzle—merely dinner.

The stories in this volume may be small in size, but remember: so are pearls. And—thanks to the playful intellects and restless imaginations of their creators—like pearls, they glow.

One of the unique encounters in the short and happy history of the Puzzle Club began, as so many interesting things do, in the most ordinary way.

That is to say, seven-thirty of that Wednesday evening found Ellery in the foyer of Syres' Park Avenue penthouse aerie pressing the bell button, having the door opened for him by a butler who had obviously been inspired by Jeeves, and being conducted into the grand-scale wood-leather-and-brass-studded living room that had just as obviously been inspired by the king-sized ranchos of the Southwest where Syres had made his millions.

As usual, Ellery found the membership assembled—with the exception, also as usual, of Arkavy, the biochemist whose Nobel achievement took him to so many international symposia that Ellery had not yet laid eyes on him; indeed, he had come to think of the great scientist as yet another fiction his fellow members had dreamed up for mischievous reasons of their own.

There was Syres himself, their hulking and profoundly respected host, respected not for being a multimillionaire but for having founded the club; tall, sardonic Darnell of the John L. Lewis eyebrows, the criminal lawyer who was known to the American bar, not altogether affectionately, as "the rich man's Clarence Darrow"; Dr. Vreeland, the psychiatrist, trim and peach-cheeked, whose professional reputation was as long as his stature was short; and wickedly blue-eyed little Emmy Wandermere, who had recently won the Pulitzer Prize for poetry to—for once—unanimous approval.

It was one of the strictest rules of the Puzzle Club that no extraneous matters—not of politics or art or economics or world affairs, or even of juicy gossip—be allowed to intrude on the business at hand, which was simply (in a manner of speaking only, since that adverb was not to be found in the club's motto) to challenge each member to solve a puzzle invented by the others, and then to repair to Charlot's dinner table, Charlot being Syres' chef, with a reputation as exalted in his field as that of the puzzlers in theirs. The puzzles were always in story form, told by the challengers *seriatim*, and they were as painstakingly planned for the battle of wits as if an empire depended on the outcome.

Tonight it was Ellery's turn again, and after the briefest of amenities he took his place in the arena, which at the Puzzle Club meant sitting down in a hugely comfortable leather chair near the super-fireplace, with a bottle, a glass, and a little buffet of Charlot's masterly canapés at hand and no further preliminaries whatever.

Darnell began (by prearrangement—the sequence of narrators was as carefully choreographed as a ballet).

"The puzzle this evening, Queen, is right down your alley—"

"Kindly omit the courtroom-type psychology, Counselor," Ellery drawled, for he was feeling in extra-fine fettle this evening, "and get on with it."

"—because it's a cops-and-robbers story," the lawyer went on, unperturbed, "except that in this case the cop is an undercover agent whose assignment it is to track down a dope supplier. The supplier is running a big wholesale illicit-drug operation; hundreds of pushers are getting their stuff from him, so it's important to nail him."

"The trouble is," Dr. Vreeland said, feeling the knot of his tie—*I wonder,* Ellery thought, *what his analyst makes of that* (it was one of the psychiatrist's most irritating habits)—"his identity is not known precisely."

"By which I take it that it's known imprecisely," Ellery said. "The unknown of a known group."

"Yes, a group of three."

"The classic number."

"It's convenient, Queen."

"That's the chief reason it's classic."

"The three suspects," oilman Syres broke in, unable to conceal a frown, for Ellery did not always comport himself with the decorum the founder thought their labors deserved, "all live in the same building. It's a three-story house."

"Someday," Ellery said, peering into the future, "instead of a three-story house, I shall make up a three-house story."

"Mr. Queen"—Emmy Wandermere let a giggle escape—"please be serious, or you won't be allowed to eat Charlot's *chef d'oeuvre,* which I understand is positively wild tonight."

"I've lost track," Syres grumped. "Where were we?"

"I beg everyone's pardon," Ellery said. "We have an undercover police officer who's turned up three suspects, one of whom is the dope wholesaler, and all three live in a three-story house, I presume one to a floor. And these habitants are?"

"The man who occupies the ground floor," the little poet replied, "and whose name is John A. Chandler—known in the neighborhood as Jac, from his initials—runs a modest one-man business, a radio-and-TV repair shop, from his apartment."

"The question is, of course," lawyer Darnell said, "whether the repair shop is just a front for the dope-supply operation."

Ellery nodded. "And the occupant of the middle floor?"

"An insurance agent," Dr. Vreeland said. "Character named Cutcliffe Kerry—"

"Named what?"

"Cutcliffe Kerry is what we decided on," the psychiatrist said firmly, "and if you don't care for it, that's your problem, Queen, because Cutcliffe Kerry he remains."

"Very well," Ellery said, "but I think I detect the aroma of fresh herring. Or am I being double-whammied? In any event,

Cutcliffe Kerry sells insurance, or tries to, which means he gets to see a great many people. So the insurance thing could be a cover. And the top floor—"

"—is rented by a fellow named Fletcher, Benjamin Fletcher," Syres said. "Fletcher is a salesman, too, but of an entirely different sort. He sells vacuum cleaners."

"Door to door," Ellery said. "Possible cover, too. All right, Jac Chandler, radio-TV repairman; Cutcliffe Kerry, insurance agent; Ben Fletcher, vacuum-cleaner salesman; and one of them is the bad guy. What happens, Mr. Syres?"

"The undercover man has been watching the building and—isn't the word *tailing*?—the three men, according to his reports to his superior at police headquarters."

"And just after he finds out who the drug supplier is," Darnell said mournfully, "but before he can come up with the hard evidence, he's murdered."

"As I suspected," Ellery said, shaking his head. "Earning the poor fellow a departmental citation and the traditional six feet of sod. He was murdered by the dope boy, of course."

"Of course."

"To shut him up."

"What else?"

"Which means he hadn't yet reported the name of the dope supplier."

"Well, not exactly, Mr. Queen." Emmy Wandermere leaned forward to accept the flame of Dr. Vreeland's gold lighter, then leaned back puffing like The Little Engine That Could on a steep grade. She was trying to curb her nicotine-and-tar intake, so she was currently smoking cigarettes made of processed lettuce. "The undercover man hadn't reported the drug supplier's name, true, but in the very last report before his murder he did mention a clue."

"What kind of clue?"

"He referred to the supplier—his subsequent killer—as, and this is an exact quote, Mr. Queen, 'the odd man of the three.'"

Ellery blinked.

"Your mission, Mr. Queen, if you accept it—and you'd better, or be kicked out of the club," said Darnell in his most doom-ridden courtroom tones, "is to detect the guilty man among Chandler, Kerry, and Fletcher—the one of them who's been selling the stuff in wholesale lots and who murdered our brave lad of the law."

"The odd man of the three, hmm?"

Ellery sat arranging his thoughts. As at all such critical stages of the game, by protocol, the strictest silence was maintained.

Finally, Ellery said, "Where and how did the murder of the undercover agent take place?"

Darnell waved his manicured hand. "Frankly, Queen, we debated whether to make up a complicated background for the crime. In the end, we decided it wouldn't be fair, because the murder itself has nothing to do with the puzzle except that it took place. The details are irrelevant and immaterial."

"Except, of course, to the victim, but that's usually left out." Having discharged himself of this philosophical gripe, Ellery resumed his seat, as it were, on his train of thought. "I suppose the premises were searched from roof to cellar, inside and out, by the police after the murder of their buddy?"

"You know it," Syres said.

"I suppose, too, that no narcotics, amphetamines, barbiturates, et cetera *ad nauseam*, no cutting equipment, no dope paraphernalia of any kind, were found anywhere in the building?"

"Not a trace," Dr. Vreeland said. "The guilty man disposed of it all before the police got there."

"Did one of the men have a record?"

Miss Wandermere smiled. "*Nyet.*"

"Was one of them a married man and were the other two bachelors?"

"No."

"Was it the other way round? One of them a bachelor and two married?"

"I admire the way you wriggle, Mr. Queen. The answer is still no."

"The odd man of the three," Ellery mused again. "Well, I see we'll have to be lexical. By the commonest definition, odd means strange, unusual, peculiar. Was there anything strange, unusual, or peculiar in, say, the appearance of Chandler or Kerry or Fletcher?"

Dr. Vreeland, with relish: "Not a thing."

"In mannerism? Behavior? Speech? Gait? That sort of thing?"

Syres: "All ordinary as hell, Queen."

"In background?"

Darnell, through a grin: "Ditto."

"There was nothing bizarre or freakish about one of them?"

"Nothing, friend," Emmy Wandermere murmured.

Ellery grasped his nose more like an enemy.

"Was one of them touched in the head?" he asked suddenly. "Odd in the mental sense?"

"There," the psychiatrist said, "you tread on muddy ground, Queen. Any antisocial behavior, as in the case of habitual criminals, might of course be so characterized. However, for purposes of our story the answer is no. All three men were normal—whatever that means."

Ellery nodded fretfully. "I could go on and on naming categories of peculiarity, but let me save us all from endangering Charlot's peace of mind. *Did* the undercover man use the word odd to connote peculiar?"

The little poet looked around and received assents invisible to the Queen eye. "He did not."

"Then that's that. Oh, one thing. Was the report in which he fingered the supplier as being 'the odd man' written or oral?"

"Now what kind of question is that?" the oil king demanded. "What could that have to do with anything?"

"Possibly a great deal, Mr. Syres. If it had been an oral report, there would be no way of knowing whether his word 'odd' began with a capital O or a small o. Assume that he'd meant it to be capital O-d-d. Then Odd man might have referred to a member of the I.O.O.F., the fraternal order of Odd Fellows. That might certainly distinguish your man from the other two."

"It was a written report," Darnell said hastily, "and the o of 'odd' was a small letter."

Everyone looked relieved. It was evident that the makers of this particular puzzle had failed to consider the Independent Order of Odd Fellows in their scheming.

"There are other 'odd' possibilities—if you'll forgive the pun—such as 'odd' in the golf meaning, which is one stroke more than your opponent has played. But I won't waste any more time on esoterica. Your undercover man meant 'odd' in the sense of 'not matching,' didn't he? Of being left over?"

"Explain that, please," Dr. Vreeland said.

"In the sense that two of the three suspects had something in common, something the third man didn't share with them—thus making the third man 'the odd man' and consequently the dope supplier and murderer. Isn't that the kind of thing your undercover agent meant by 'odd man'?"

The psychiatrist looked cautious. "I think we may fairly say yes to that."

"Thank you very much," Ellery said. "Which brings me to a fascinating question: How clever are you people being? Run-of-the-game clever or clever-clever?"

"I don't think," Miss Wandermere said, "we quite follow. What do you mean exactly, Mr. Queen?"

"Did you intend to give me a choice of solutions? The reason I ask is that I see not one possible answer, but three."

"Three!" Syres shook his massive head. "We had enough trouble deciding on one."

"I, for one," Counselor Darnell stated stiffishly, "should like to hear a for-instance."

"All right, I'll give you one solution I doubt you had in mind, since it's so obvious."

"You know, Queen, you have a sadistic streak in you?" barked Dr. Vreeland. "Obvious! Which solution is obvious?"

"Why, Doctor. Take the names of two of your suspects, John A.— Jac—Chandler and Benjamin Fletcher. Oddly enough—there I go again!—those surnames have two points of similarity. Chandler and Fletcher both end in 'er,' and both contain eight letters. Cutcliffe Kerry's surname differs in both respects—no 'er' ending and only five letters—so Kerry becomes the odd surname of the trio. In this solution, then, Kerry the insurance man is the supplier-killer."

"I'll be damned," Syres exclaimed. "How did we miss that?"

"Very simply," Miss Wandermere said. "We didn't see it."

"Never mind that," Darnell snapped. "The fact is it happened. Queen, you said you have three solutions. What's another?"

"Give me a clue to the solution you people had in mind, since there are more than one. Some key word that indicates the drift but doesn't give the game away. One word can do it."

Syres, Darnell, and Dr. Vreeland jumped up and surrounded Emmy Wandermere. From their looped figures, cocked heads, and murderous whispers, they might have been the losing team in an offensive huddle with six seconds left to play. Finally, the men resumed their seats, nudging one another.

Said little Miss Wandermere: "You asked for a clue, Mr. Queen. The clue is: *clue*."

Ellery threw his head back and roared. "Right! Very clever, considering who I am and that I'm the solver of the evening.

"You hurled my specialized knowledge in my teeth, calculating that I'd be so close to it I wouldn't see it. Sorry! Two of the surnames you invented," Ellery said with satisfaction, "are of famous detective-story writers. Chandler—in this case Raymond Chandler—was the widely acclaimed creator of Philip Marlowe. Joseph Smith Fletcher—J. S. Fletcher—produced more detective fiction than any other writer except Edgar Wallace, or so it's said; Fletcher's *The Middle Temple Murder* was publicly praised by no lesser mystery fan than the President of the United States, Woodrow Wilson. On the other hand, if there's ever been a famous detective-story writer named Cutcliffe Kerry, his fame has failed to reach me. So your Mr. Kerry again becomes the odd man of the trio and the answer to the problem. Wasn't that your solution, Miss Wandermere and gentlemen?"

They said yes in varying tones of chagrin.

Ordinarily at this point in the evening's proceedings, the company would have risen from their chairs and made for Syres' magnificently gussied-up cookhouse of a dining room. But tonight no one stirred a toe, not even at the promise of the manna simmering on Charlot's hob. Instead, Dr. Vreeland uttered a small, inquiring cough.

"You, ah, mentioned a third solution, Queen. Although I must confess—"

"Before you pronounce your *mea culpa*, Doctor," Ellery said with a smile, "may I? I've given you people your solution. I've even thrown in another for good measure. Turn-about? I now challenge you. What's the third solution?"

CHALLENGE TO THE READER

What is the third solution?

THE SOLUTION

Ten minutes later, Ellery showed them mercy—really, he said sorrowfully, more in the interest of preserving Charlot's chancy goodwill than out of natural goodness of heart.

"John A. Chandler, Cutcliffe Kerry, Benjamin Fletcher. Chandler, Kerry, and Fletcher. What do two of these have in common, besides what's already been discussed? Why, they derive from trades or occupations."

"Chandler." The lawyer, Darnell, looked around at the others, startled. "You know, that's true!"

"Yes, a ship chandler deals in specified goods or equipment. If you go farther back in time, you find that a chandler was someone who made or sold candles, or, as in very early England, supervised the candle requirements of a household. So that's one trade.

"Now, is there another in the remaining two surnames?

"Yes. A fletcher was—and technically still is—a maker of arrows, or a dealer in same; in the Middle Ages, by extension, although this was a rare meaning, the word was sometimes used to denote an archer. In either case, another trade or occupation.

"But the only etymological origin I've ever heard ascribed to the name Kerry is County Kerry, from which the Kerry blue terrier derives. And that's not a trade, it's a place. So, with the names Chandler and Fletcher going back to occupations and Kerry to Irish geography, your Mr. Kerry becomes once again the unpaired meaning, the 'odd man'—a third answer to your problem."

And Ellery rose and offered his arm gallantly to Miss Wandermere.

The poetess took it with a little shake. And as they led the way to the feast she whispered, "You know what you are, Ellery Queen? You're an intellectual *pack rat!*"

THE HONEST SWINDLER

originally published in *The Saturday Evening Post* (Summer 1971)

INTRODUCTION BY RICHARD DANNAY:

Queen fans are familiar with Anthony Boucher's oft-quoted opinion that "Ellery Queen is *the American detective story." They may be less familiar with the opinion of Isaac Asimov that "Fred Dannay . . . probably did more for the mystery field than any other single person since Conan Doyle" (in* Banquets of the Black Widowers, *Ballantine Books, 1986, p. 129).*

In that lofty context, where do the five Puzzle Club stories fit? Just fun and games? It would be easy to view these short pure puzzles as the distillation, the golden nugget, of Queen's love of the ingenious fair-play detective story. As John Dickson Carr asked in his famous essay on the detective story, "The Grandest Game in the World" (EQMM, March 1963), "What, after all, is the game itself?" His answer: "It is a hoodwinking contest, a duel between author and reader." Indeed, each of the final three Puzzle Club stories contains the "Challenge to the Reader" that appeared in most of the early Queen novels, that interlude where readers were told they had all the facts essential to a clear solution of the mystery and were invited to match wits with Ellery Queen.

But the fictional Puzzle Club membership itself provides at least two clues about my father that may be less obvious to readers: one member, Emmy Wandermere, is a poet, while another, Dr. Vreeland, is a psychiatrist.

Why a poet? Why a psychiatrist?

My father, in the 1967 Queen anthology Poetic Justice *(with prose contributions from Chaucer to Dylan Thomas), explained what he considered "the marriage of poetry and mystery" as follows: "Poets bring order out of chaos. Detectives, in resolving mysteries, also bring order out of chaos. Things equal to the same thing are equal to each other. Therefore poets are detectives, and detectives are poets. Q.E.D."*

Okay, then, but why a psychiatrist? When my father was a guest on The Dick Cavett Show *in 1978, in recognition of the fiftieth anniversary of Ellery Queen, Cavett asked him what he might have done had he not become a writer. Not hesitating, he said his first choice (before artist and actor) was psychiatrist, explaining that he was a "born snoop" and "interested in the secret lives of people."*

Q.E.D.

"Who leads off this evening?" asked Ellery. It was his turn to crack the mystery.

"My gambit." Syres was the founder of the Puzzle Club. The regular meetings took place in his Park Avenue penthouse, and his chef s *cordon bleu* dinners were never served until the challenged member had either triumphed or failed. So a hungry Ellery took the inquisitional armchair facing four of his five co-members—the fifth, Arkavy the Nobel biochemist, was in Glasgow attending one of his interfering symposiums —and was fortifying himself from the steam tray of Charlot's canapé works of art.

"The villain of tonight's puzzle," began the multimillionaire, who had made his oily pile in the Southwest, "is an old scamp, one of those legendary prospectors the West used to brag could live for months on beans and jerky in temperatures that would frazzle an ordinary man's gizzard or turn his blood to mush-ice."

"Old Pete's life," Darnell, the criminal lawyer, took up the tale, "has been one uninterrupted washout. Although he's tracked a hundred El Dorado-type rumors thousands of miles in his time, he's never once made the big strike. Only an occasional miserable stake scratched out of hard-pan has kept Pete alive. Doctor?"

The psychiatrist, Vreeland, tapped the ash surgically off his two- dollar cigar. "Finally the mangy old fox becomes desperate. Frustration, loneliness, advancing years have whittled his wits to a fine edge; he plots a cunning—no, why plagiarize the shrinking violet? a brilliant!— scheme. To carry it off, he sells just about everything in the world he owns. It brings him enough to pay for a display ad in *The Wall Street Journal*."

"*The Wall Street Journal*?" Ellery helped himself to the Scotch, looking delighted. "What imagination, what panache! Exactly how does your villain word his ad, by the way?"

Little Emmy Wandermere, who had just won the Pulitzer Prize for poetry, offered him a sheet of paper. On it she had penciled in her swashy hand:

Finance My Uranium Hunt!
Impossible to Lose!!
5-Year Money-Back Guarantee!
Complete Refund Even If Uranium Is Never Found!
Old Prospector, Box 1313

"Hardly a *Wall Street Journal*-type ad," Ellery said. "I'll put it down to poet's license, Miss Wandermere. And the response to Pete's pitch?"

"Heavy," the oil tycoon said. "You know what I always say—a sure thing gathers no moss. The dough comes rolling in."

"Can you give me a figure, Mr. Syres?"

"Well, let's say five hundred suckers invest one hundred dollars each to stake the old skunk for five years. That's fifty thousand dollars. Agreeable, Miss Wandermere, gentlemen?"

The poet, the lawyer, and the psychiatrist nodded solemnly.

"In short, Mr. Queen," Dr. Vreeland said, "if Pete should strike uranium, the investors can realize many times their investments."

"Would you believe like five thousand percent on their money?" winked the oilman.

"But even if he should fail," Lawyer Darnell chipped in, "every last investor at least gets back his original investment. That was Pete's offer."

"Do you mean that if I'd staked Pete to a hundred dollars of my money and he didn't find uranium, he'd give me my hundred back?"

"Your money, and that of every other investor."

Ellery meditated. The company waited. Finally Ellery said, "Did the old fellow find uranium, or didn't he?"

"If I may embroider the obvious, gentlemen?" The lady-poet's wicked blue eyes took on a faraway look. "Prospector Pete, better provisioned and outfitted than he's ever been outside his most beautiful dreams, sets out on his uranium quest. With the euphoria of his breed, he spends years—in the deserts, the plains, the mountains, the glaciers, from Baja California, to the Rockies to Alaska and all stops between—patient years of foot-slogging, climbing, chipping, digging, panning, or whatever it is you do when you're looking for uranium. The sun fries him, the rain waterlogs him, snow and ice make a Father Frost out of him. Many times he nearly dies of thirst. He runs the risks of bear and cougar and, worst of all, of loneliness. It does seem as if he deserves a happy ending, Mr. Queen, but he doesn't get it. He finds absolutely nothing. Not a squawk or a wiggle in his Geiger counter. Until finally the time limit in his guarantee is up, and he hasn't a cent left."

"Whereupon," Syres said, "old Pete makes good the promise in his ad."

To which Darnell added, with magnificent simplicity, "End of story."

There was a tranquil hush.

"Well," Ellery muttered. "I see. His money's gone, he's failed to find uranium, and still he manages to pay back every one of his backers. In full?"

"In full."

"Then and there? Not ten years later?"

"Within twenty-four hours," Dr. Vreeland said. "Question: How does Pete do it?"

"I suppose I had better rule out the obvious. He hadn't found something else of value? Gold, say? Diamonds? Platinum?"

Emmy Wandermere looked sad. "Alas, as they used to say, Mr. Queen. He found nothing."

"Or just before the five years were up, his long-lost uncle—on his mother's side, of course—died in Poona, Illinois, and left him ten billion *lakhs*?"

"Please," Lawyer Darnell said, pained. "Our man Pete is penniless when he runs the ad, his prospecting efforts produce an unrelieved zero, he doesn't have an uncle, and at the expiration of the five years he can't claim a single negotiable asset. His equipment is worn out and not worth the match to set it on fire, and even his burro has died of exhaustion."

"Yet every investor gets his money back *in toto.*"

"Every investor, every dollar."

"Hm," Ellery said, reaching for the Scotch again.

"You have the usual one hour, Queen," Syres said briskly. "After that, as you know, Charlot's dinner—"

"Yes, won't be edible, and I'm declared Nitwit of the Month." Ellery took an elegant swallow. "To avert both disasters, I'd better solve your puzzle right now."

CHALLENGE TO THE READER

How did old Pete manage to repay the entire fifty thousand dollars after five years, in spite of his failure to find anything of value and winding up dead broke?

THE SOLUTION

"The answer has to be," Ellery said gently, "that *he never touched the fifty thousand dollars in the first place.* Didn't spend a dime of it. So when the time limit expired, he was naturally able to give the whole sum back.

"But if he never touched the principal, how did he manage to finance five years of prospecting?

"Simplest way in the world," Ellery went on. "When he first collected the fifty thousand dollars from his backers, he deposited the entire amount in a savings bank. At, say, five percent interest, the fifty thousand dollars would bring him an income of twenty-five hundred dollars a year. Twenty-five hundred dollars a year was a sumptuous grubstake to a desert rat with one ancient burro to his name and a lifetime's practice in living on next to nothing.

"Old Pete was no swindler, and he certainly wasn't the scoundrel you deliberately painted him to set me off the track. He was simply a businessman following time-honored business practice. And now, fellow-puzzlers, shall we partake of Charlot's goodies?"

Ellery flourished his empty glass. "I'm ready to eat Pete's burro."

PART II

THE PASTICHES

by Josh Pachter

A STUDY IN *SCARLETT!*

originally published in *Ellery Queen's Mystery Magazine* (May/June 2019)

INTRODUCTION BY JANET HUTCHINGS:

I am, in a sense, the outlier amongst those contributing to this book. Josh Pachter's introduction hinted at this when he recounted my reluctance to commit to a series of Puzzle Club pastiches. It's not that I'm indisposed towards Ellery Queen pastiches in general—on the contrary, it's always a pleasure for me to see someone bring these characters I've enjoyed so much to life again. It's simply that I was not, when Josh broached the subject, a particular fan of the puzzle-club format (which is, of course, not the format for most of the original Ellery Queen stories). For me, the problem with the puzzle-club (or dinner-table) mystery has always been that in such stories the reader is rarely allowed to enter vicariously into the story. We aren't witnessing the unfolding of the murder or its aftermath or its investigation. Instead, we're presented with a summary and a discussion of it—and we're often explicitly reminded that it isn't a real *murder or puzzle. As a result, the experience is predominantly intellectual; rarely are our sympathies engaged or emotions excited. As Emmy Wandermere says in the story you're about to read, in answer to Ellery's question "Why not simply write the name of her killer, rather than resorting to this cryptic rigmarole?": "She didn't simply write the name, my dear sleuth, because, had she done so, there wouldn't be a puzzle for you to solve!"*

If I am not a natural-born fan of this subgenre of the mystery—as I suspect most of the other contributors to this volume are—Josh's charming Puzzle Club stories have, nevertheless, made me something of a convert. His light touch, his clever word plays, his own clear love of the form have all proved as compelling to me as I'm sure they will to other readers. When the final story in the series, "Their Last Bow," came along, I was sorry the curtain was closing. I don't know quite how Josh has managed it in a series of stories of under 3,000 words in which nearly every word is employed in delineation of a puzzle and its solution, but somehow he's brought to distinctive new life the characters from the original series. As for his puzzles themselves, they're genuinely challenging, especially this first one, which isn't based on any specialized knowledge but on something I'm still willing to bet you won't decipher before Ellery.

It had been years since the club's last meeting—decades!—and the gray-haired gentleman with his finger on the buzzer beside the penthouse aerie's oaken door had feared that one of its six members must have died.

But then, out of the blue, the invitation had come, and he had endured with mounting impatience and excitement the week between its arrival and the appointed day and time, had at last pulled his soup-and-fish out of mothballs and taken a cab to the Park Avenue skyscraper he remembered so fondly.

The door was opened by a young man in butler's livery—a man young enough that, at the time of the club's last meeting, he must have been in diapers ... if he had by then been alive at all. It was impossible that the elderly gentleman had ever encountered this particular servant before, and yet recognition flickered at the back of his mind. "And you are?" he enquired, placing his card on the proffered silver salver.

"Charles, sir," the butler said, pronouncing it "Sharl", *a la Française*, and at that moment the penny dropped.

"You don't mean to say—!"

"Indeed, sir. Charlot is my father."

"*Is*? You mean he's—"

"—still with us? Yes, sir, he is. Long retired, of course, but he's back in the kitchen this evening, preparing one last feast for Mr. Syres and his guests. This way, sir."

He followed the butler down the familiar corridor, enjoying as always the incredible art collection that decorated its walls on both sides. The young man held the library door for him, and the elderly gentleman stepped through it into what had been the scene of some of his most satisfying—though certainly least important—

triumphs.

And there they were.

Syres himself—owner of the penthouse and so much more, a multimillionaire who had made his fortune in the oil fields of the Southwest—was in a wheelchair now, and his gnarled hands trembled with Parkinson's. The man must be ninety if he was a day.

Clustered around him stood the other three:

Darnell, the criminal defense attorney known far and wide—and not altogether affectionately—as "the rich man's Clarence Darrow."

Vreeland, the diminutive psychiatrist.

And little Emmy Wandermere, the Pulitzer Prize-winning poet, every bit as old as their host, though still vertical and apparently mobile.

Then a stranger emerged from the shadows in a corner of the room, a fireplug of a man with a shiny bald dome and a bushy white beard and an unlit cigar, and the elderly gentleman blinked in surprise at the sight of the unfamiliar face before finally realizing who it was—who it *had* to be.

"Professor Arkavy, I presume?"

Anatoly Arkavy had been a member of this strange association since its initial meeting, but his Nobel in chemistry had made him such a sought-after speaker at international symposia that this was in fact the first time the two of them had ever had occasion to meet.

"Indeed I am," the scientist said, gripping the elderly gentleman's hand and shaking it vigorously. "And you must be the famous Ellery Queen. I've heard a lot about you, sir. Our fellow Puzzle Clubbians have been singing your praises."

Charles appeared at Ellery's side and handed him a scotch and soda.

"Now that Anatoly has achieved emeritus status and left the Halls of Academe behind him," said the wiry old man in the wheelchair, his voice hoarse with age, "I thought it would be pleasant to have at long last a meeting all six of us could attend."

"Before one of us croaks," said Miss Wandermere.

"Poetically put," Dr. Vreeland smiled.

Arkavy sipped his bourbon. "I'm eager to see, Mr. Queen, if you live up to your reputation."

"From which I deduce," said Ellery, "that I have been elected to take the hot seat this evening?"

"By unanimous acclamation," Darnell nodded.

The elderly gentleman began to protest that the acclamation could hardly have been unanimous, since he himself had not been consulted, but he swallowed first his objection and then a healthy helping of highball and settled into the overstuffed Chesterfield that, in Puzzle Club parlance, was known as the "Problem Chair," with a plate of Charlot's succulent canapés at his side.

"Without further ado," Syres began, "I take you to the Sherbert Theater on West 47th Street—"

"You mean the Shubert on West 44th," Ellery interrupted.

"I most certainly do *not*," the oilman wheezed. "When I'm in the Problem Chair and you're telling the story, you can set it wherever you damn well please, El. But *this* story takes place in the refreshingly air-conditioned *Sherbert* Theater on West Forty-Seventh Street, three blocks north of the Shubert. May I proceed?"

The elderly gentleman took an embarrassed sip of his drink.

"*Harrumph*," said Syres. "Now, as I was saying, in the Sherbert Theater on 47th Street, just a few steps west of Broadway and Times Square, the curtain is about to go up on the final dress rehearsal for *Scarlett!*, the third attempt to adapt Margaret Mitchell's classic *Gone With the Wind* as a musical."

"The set gleams beneath the Fresnel lights," the poetess picked up the recitation, "the orchestra is halfway through the overture, the cast is assembled on stage ... but wait! Oh, where, oh, where has Brooke Rivers, the twenty-something starlet who—fresh off her success as Cecily Cardew in the umpteenth revival of *The Importance of Being Earnest*—has been cast in the role of Scarlett O'Hara, gone? Oh, where, oh, where can she be?"

"A flunky is dispatched backstage to find her," Dr. Vreeland went on, "and find her, he does—in her dressing room, slumped over her vanity, quite dead, stabbed in the back, surrounded by lipsticks and creams and tubes and bottles and jars, but also by books of crosswords, cryptics, acrostics, word searches, logic problems—"

"Puzzle books," Ellery interjected.

"Puzzle books," Professor Arkavy confirmed. "It seems that, in her off-hours, Miss Rivers was quite the devotee of word games in all their forms. She had even contributed several puzzles of her own design to various magazines."

"—and, as I say," Vreeland went on, "in the midst of all this makeup and puzzlement lies a single sheet of heavy cream-colored writing paper, on which five words have been neatly hand-printed, to wit: ABCESS, DEFEATED, NEIGHING, HIJACK, INOPERABLE. Beneath them, a sixth word has been hastily scrawled: FOUR."

"F-O-U-R," asked Ellery, "or F-O-R, or F-O-R-E?"

"Not the preposition," Miss Wandermere replied, "and not the golfer's warning, but the number, F-O-U-R."

Darnell the attorney cleared his throat. "The dress rehearsal is cancelled, of course, and the police are called in. Leading the investigation is, shall we say, Inspector Richard Queen of the NYPD."

"By all means," said Ellery. "Let's say that. And I suppose there are the usual three suspects?"

"Actually," Arkavy replied, "in honor of my presence at this evening's gathering, we have added one extra suspect to our cast of characters."

"So, *four*," Ellery murmured. "And may I assume that each of the four of them had a motive for murdering Our Miss Brooke?"

"No need to assume," said the poetess. "That just makes an ass of you and me. The fact is that each of the four suspects *did* have a strong motive to help Miz Scahlett shuffle off this mortal coil."

"First," said Syres, "we have Max Rubinstein, the producer of *Scarlett!* He was a very successful impresario back home in Poland, but his first two American efforts lost money, and he's counting on *Scarlett!* to put him back in the black. The rehearsals, however, have been plagued with difficulty, and Max is concerned that the show will be a flop. But he's insured his starlet's life for a cool three million dollars, and her death will help offset the money he's concerned he's about to lose."

"Second," Darnell took up the narrative, "is Ian Kent, the handsome actor playing Rhett Butler. He's had a string of hit movies, but this is his first theatrical role. He hated his costar because she was constantly upstaging him, ad-libbing suggestive remarks that made him seem ridiculous."

"Third," continued Vreeland smoothly, "allow me to introduce you to Ronald 'Buzz' Berkeley, the—"

"Buzz?" Ellery demurred.

"He's the hottest choreographer on Broadway at the moment, a twenty-first century Busby Berkeley—though no relation to his twentieth century namesake."

Ellery waved him on.

"Unfortunately," the psychiatrist continued, "Brooke Rivers consistently refuses to dance the steps he's designed for her and insists on substituting her own amateurish moves, which throws the rest of his choreography out of whack and infuriates him to the point of—well, perhaps of murder?"

"Fourth and finally," concluded little Emmy Wandermere, "we have Katherine Higgins, Brooke's understudy, known to one and all as Kat. No timid kitten, though, is this particular Kat: she's well aware that Brooke has never missed a single performance in her illustrious though brief career, which means that Kat Higgins sees no chance of showing the world what she can do ... as long as the star of *Scarlett!* remains alive. And there you have them, my dear boy, in all their glory."

As Ellery nibbled thoughtfully at a shrimp puff, Charles appeared with a tray and freshened their drinks.

Syres leaned forward in his wheelchair. "With Charlot's excellent meal in the oven," he said, "you have the traditional one hour, El, to arrive at a solution."

The elderly gentleman tented his fingers and went to work. "To begin," he said, "what was the late Miss Rivers stabbed with?"

Darnell shook off the question. "Irrelevant and immaterial."

"Call it a sharpened eyebrow pencil," grinned Miss Wandermere. "Next question?"

"Were the six words on the sheet of notepaper written by the dead woman?"

"They were," said Arkavy.

"With a sharpened eyebrow pencil," cackled Miss Wandermere. "Next?"

"Does any of the four suspects have dental problems? Is one of them afflicted with a terminal illness? Does one have an equine laugh?"

"You're neighing up the wrong tree, Queen," said the psychiatrist. "No ABCESS. Nothing INOPERABLE. And a resounding nay to NEIGHING."

"Is it safe to conclude, then, that the first five words Brooke Rivers wrote were *not* our obligatory dying message, that her actual message was the sixth word, the hastily scrawled FOUR?"

"Safe!" Syres shouted, his trembling hands sweeping outward like an umpire at home plate.

"So the key word here is FOUR," Ellery mused, "and there are four suspects. Was she saying that all four of them killed her?"

"Tish tosh," said Emmy Wandermere, "'ave you forgotten 'Erbert 'All, the Cockney Uncle from Australia, 'oos dying word hultimately meant that 'is niece and two nephews 'ad '*hall*' conspired to murder 'im?"

"Give us some credit, Ellery," Darnell said. "We're quite familiar with your exploits in the real world outside the Puzzle Club, and we're not about to lead you down a garden path you've already traveled."

"All right, then, which *one* of them does the dying message indicate? The number four points in many possible directions. The Four Gospels of Christianity, the Four Matriarchs of Judaism, the Four Noble Truths of Buddhism." He hesitated. "Noble. Nobel. It's not going to turn out that *you* killed her, Professor Arkavy?"

The biochemist pursed his lips. "Hardly, Mr. Queen. I assure you that the guilty party was one of the four suspects we've identified."

"One of the four. The *four*. There are four dimensions of time and space, four movements in a symphony, four houses of Hogwarts in the world of Harry Potter."

"I love those books," Emmy Wandermere beamed.

"Four suits in a deck of cards, four score and seven years ago, the Fourth Estate, Four Corners in the American Southwest, Marvel's Fantastic Four, Liverpool's Fab Four—"

"I *love* those Beatles," Emmy Wandermere gushed.

"Four is the atomic number of beryllium and the only cardinal numeral that has the same number of letters in the English language as its number value. I could go on—"

"—and on," said Darnell drily.

"—but I'll spare you. Let's get down to brass tacks, instead. Each of our four suspects has a direct personal connection with the number four. Ian Kent is the only one of them with a four-letter last name, and 'Buzz' Berkeley is the only one with a four-letter first name—or, rather, nickname. Based on what you've told me, Max Rubinstein is the only suspect who emigrated to the United States from elsewhere, making him the only—"

"Don't say it!" Syres groaned.

"How can I not? He's the only *for*eigner in the bunch. And Katherine Higgins? Well, this is also a bit of a stretch, but the French word for four is—"

"*Quatre*," Arkavy and Vreeland supplied in unison, both of them pronouncing it correctly as "Kat."

"By the by," asked Ellery, "why did she spell out the number FOUR? Why not write the numeral, instead? And why," he continued, a twinkle in his eye, "not simply write the name of her killer, rather than resorting to this cryptic rigamarole?"

"Well," Darnell the lawyer began, "she knew that it was possible the killer might return to the dressing room and find the—"

"Oh, fiddle-de-dee," Miss Wandermere scoffed. "She didn't simply write the name, my dear sleuth, because, had she done so, there wouldn't be a puzzle for you to solve!"

"And remember," Arkavy put in, "that the dead woman was fascinated by puzzles. Surely she wouldn't have wanted to make things easy on your poor father the inspector."

"Or on you," added Syres.

"Point taken." Ellery sipped his highball, checked his watch, rubbed a hand across his chin. And then he closed his eyes and sat there, deep in thought.

The millionaire slapped the arms of his wheelchair with delight. "Have we defeated you at last, El? Have we finally come up with a problem that even the great Ellery Queen can't puzzle out?"

And then Ellery's eyes opened wide.

"By George," said Anatoly Arkavy, "I think he's got it."

Challenge to the Reader

Who killed Brooke Rivers? And how did Ellery know?

THE SOLUTION

"Brooke Rivers loved puzzles," Ellery said. "She'd even contributed a number of them to the sort of magazines that littered her dressing-room vanity, and the five words she'd neatly written on that piece of stationery were the beginnings of a puzzle she was working on just before she was killed."

He paused to drain the last drops of his highball, then went on. "ABCESS, DEFEATED, NEIGHING, HIJACK, and INOPERABLE. What puzzling feature do those five words have in common? Simple: each of them contains three consecutive letters that appear consecutively and in the same order in the alphabet: the ABC of ABCESS, the DEF of DEFEATED, the GHI of NEIGHING, the HIJ of HIJACK, and the NOP of INOPERABLE."

"I'll be damned," said Dr. Vreeland, "he *has* got it."

Ellery smiled. "Brooke's scrawled FOUR told the police to look for a word which contains *four* consecutive letters that appear consecutively and in the same order in the alphabet—and there is only one such word in the English language. The murderer," Ellery said, "was Katherine Higgins, Brooke Rivers' jealous UNDERSTUDY."

There was a momentary silence.

Then Professor Arkavy set his unlit cigar down in a crystal ashtray and slowly began to applaud. "I'm pleased to see," he said, "that the reports of your depth have *not* been greatly exaggerated."

As if on cue, a gong sounded, and Charles announced that dinner was served.

Ellery got to his feet and attempted to assist little Emmy Wandermere to hers. But she pushed him away and punched his shoulder. "I thought we finally had you stumped." She scowled.

"Well, now that the Puzzle Club seems to have reconvened after its long hiatus, perhaps you'll have another chance." He took her by the elbow and led her into the dining room, where Charlot's feast awaited.

"After all," Ellery Queen grinned, "tomorrow *is* another day."

THE ADVENTURE OF THE RED CIRCLES

originally published in *Ellery Queen's Mystery Magazine* (January/February 2020)

INTRODUCTION BY ARTHUR VIDRO:

Most of the kids I grew up with wanted to be Superman or Wonder Woman, but not me. I wanted to be a television detective.

Unfortunately, I lacked Mannix's ability to fight. I didn't have Rockford's gumption or Barnaby Jones' marksmanship. I couldn't join the Hawaii 5-0 *team, because I wasn't strong enough to pass a police physical.*

But how about Ellery Queen? I couldn't be the Ellery who starred in the EQ novels: I didn't have a relative on the police to involve me in cases, and Ellery's worldly sophistication and wealth were out of my reach.

Then I stumbled upon the Puzzle Club, a lesser-known segment of the Queen canon. These five tales, written toward the end of the Dannay-Lee collaboration, were admittedly not as complex or brilliant as the earlier masterpieces, but they held for me a special appeal: they featured an Ellery Queen I was able to emulate.

The Puzzle Club's Ellery didn't solve real-life crimes alongside his father or unravel mysteries he stumbled upon in his travels.

No, he merely met with fellow lovers and concocters of puzzles to sip drinks and engage in battles of wits to solve purely fictitious crimes.

That was something I felt that even I could do.

Therefore, it's a pleasure for me to see the original quintet of Puzzle Club stories—which are hard to find individually—brought together in one volume at last, and an extra treat to have them joined by the five pastiches penned by Josh Pachter, whose own Puzzle Club tales are every bit as engaging as the originals.

"The Adventure of the Red Circles" starts with a truly funny joke,

mentions Djuna (the houseboy in the Queen household), includes a typical Queenian dying-message clue, has Ellery "murmur" once (I'll wager EQ "murmured" at least once in each of his books), and even references Inspector Queen's right-hand man, Sergeant Thomas Velie.

Best of all, the victim in this story is a book lover and collector, surrounded by shelves of first-edition Golden Age detective novels, a setting that made me feel right at home. I read it surrounded by my own carefully organized Carr, Christie, and Queen collections, wondering if the "best detectives" assigned to investigate the suspects' alibis might perhaps have been named Flint, Hagstrom, Hesse, Johnson, Piggott, and Ritter....

"Two chemists walk into a bar," said Anatoly Arkavy in his thick Russian accent, waving an unlit cigar to emphasize his words, "and the bartender says, 'Greetings, gents, what can I do you for?' The first chemist ponders a moment and says, 'I believe I'll have a glass of H_2O.' 'Coming right up,' says the bartender, and he serves the man some water. The second chemist says, 'I suppose I'll have a glass of H_2O, too.' The bartender looks a bit skeptical, but he fills the order—and the second chemist *dies*."

Only Ellery Queen laughed. The four other people in the room—Syres the multimillionaire, Vreeland the psychiatrist, Darnell the attorney, Emmy Wandermere the poet—simply stared at the bearded bald biochemist in mystified silence.

"The second chemist asked for H_2O_2," Ellery explained. "That's hydrogen peroxide. It's a strong oxidizing agent used to treat infections when applied topically, but a deadly poison when ingested."

"So you're saying the bartender was *also* a chemist?" asked Darnell. "Then why did he serve the poor man a drink he knew would kill him?"

"Did he know the second chemist from somewhere?" Vreeland said. "Did he have a motive for the murder?"

"*Chert poberi*," Arkavy sighed. "What's wrong with you people? This isn't tonight's puzzle. It's a *joke*."

"Ah," said Emmy Wandermere soberly. "A joke. Ha ha, then."

Syres, their host, rapped his empty glass sharply on the arm of his wheelchair. He was the founder of the Puzzle Club and, at ninety, the oldest member of the group by fifteen years. "Speaking of tonight's puzzle," he wheezed, "I have, as you know, managed to coax Charlot out of retirement to prepare another of his sumptuous meals for us, and we wouldn't want it to be spoilt, so perhaps we'd best get down to cases. El, you're in the hot seat this evening, and I believe you'll find the conundrum we've cooked up for you particularly tasty."

Ellery took his seat in the overstuffed Chesterfield the members of the Puzzle Club affectionately referred to as the Problem Chair and swallowed the last of his Scotch and soda, and Charles the butler appeared at his side and presented him with a new one on a silver tray.

Dr. Vreeland cleared his throat and began the evening's story. "Jeremiah 'Red' Edwards is the owner of two dozen Big Red's Inns, a very successful chain of Long Island grocery stores," he said. "Once upon a time, his hair color gave rise to his nickname, but now, in his late fifties, he has, alas, gone completely bald—rather like our good friend Professor Arkavy. Unlike the professor, however, he has also gone completely *dead*, apparently a suicide, with a single gunshot wound in his chest and a small-caliber revolver still clutched in his right hand."

"And before you rabbit off on a wild-goose chase, my dear boy," put in Miss Wandermere, the strength of her mixed drink perhaps accounting for the weakness of her mixed metaphor, "let me assure you that Dead Red *was* in fact right-handed and not a southpaw."

"Thank you, Emmy," Vreeland nodded. "I should have said so myself. To continue, Red's body is found slumped over his desk in the library of his sprawling estate in the appropriately named incorporated village of Muttontown by his manservant—"

"Jeeves?" said Ellery tentatively.

The psychiatrist frowned. "I was going to say Djuna in your honor, Queen, but why not? Jeeves it is." He sipped his martini and resumed the recitation. "As I say, he is found in his library by his manservant, Jeeves, surrounded by his extensive collection of rare first editions of Golden Age detective novels: the library's bookshelves are filled with the works of John Dickson Carr, Agatha

Christie, G.K. Chesterton, S.S. Van Dine—and, oh, yes, a certain Ellery Queen."

"When the medical examiner has completed his *in situ* examination of the body and the *corpus* has been carted off to the morgue," Darnell took over, "the investigating homicide detectives find a red grease pencil and the proofs for next week's Big Red's advertising circular lying on his desk, where the dead man's body had previously hidden them from view. Red's weekly habit, Jeeves informs them, is to mark up the proofs with the grease pencil, and he has in fact done so with the first pages of this layout. But the document is folded open to the page featuring specials from the cheese department, and, on this particular page, instead of his usual additions and deletions and corrections, Red has circled the photographs of four of the items on offer and numbered them one to four, in the following order: a sixteen-ounce jar of grated Romano marked down from $12.99 to $10.49, an eight-ounce Brie round for $6.49, a five-ounce wedge of smoked Gouda for $7.95, and a four-ounce tub of feta crumbles at two for $7.39. At the bottom of the page, in the otherwise blank margin, the dead man has drawn a fifth red circle, inside which he has scrawled the numeral five."

"Our first question, of course," said Syres, "is, *was* he in fact a suicide, or was he murdered?"

"I'll give you a hint," said the poetess. "He was murdered."

"But in true dying-message-story fashion," the millionaire continued, "he survived long enough after being shot to circle and number the four cheeses on the proof sheet and add an additional fifth circle and number as a cryptic means of identifying his killer. And—don't be shocked, now—there are three suspects. First—"

"*Ladies* first!" Miss Wandermere cut in. "After all, *cherchez la femme* and all that. The most obvious suspect is Red's wife, Emily. She's been carrying on with the gardener, an immigrant from Cairo, and wants a divorce so she can marry him. Sadly, Emily hasn't got a dime of her own money and Achmed is not merely dimeless but penniless. Red, of course, wouldn't divorce—so the best way to the money's to murder her honey."

"This is what got you a Pulitzer?" murmured Ellery.

"Suspect Number Two," said Anatoly Arkavy, "is Red and Emily's son, Edward. The name was Red's idea, and being stuck with the name Edward Edwards might perhaps have been motive enough for him to shoot his father all by itself, but there's more. Young Edward is, you see, an inveterate gambler—and, more to the point, an inveterate loser. He is deeply in debt to his bookie, who is threatening to break one or more of his most important appendages if his account isn't satisfactorily settled. Edward begged his father to bail him out of this awful situation, but Red flat-out refused."

"And Edward, like Emily, inherits in the event of Red's demise?"

"Equally, fifty-fifty. And we're talking *millions* here, Mr. Queen. There's apparently quite a bit of cabbage in the grocery business."

"Third and finally," said Darnell, "we have Albertson Kroger, the owner of a competing chain of stores. He's been losing market share to Big Red's in recent months, and he would be thrilled to see his main competitor's empire thrown into the sort of turmoil that would inevitably result from the death of its owner."

"The police have checked to see if each of them has an alibi?" asked Ellery.

"Indeed they have, and Inspector Velie—"

"No, really?"

"No, *Velie,* Inspector Thomas Velie. By an odd coincidence, his father used to work for *your* father in the olden days. He has assigned his best detectives to the alibis of the three suspects, and each of them seems to be iron-clad."

"And there you have it, El," said Syres. "You're entitled to the usual one hour to ask questions. Would you like to begin with the details of the three alibis?"

"Oh," said Ellery, "I don't need to ask any questions, and I couldn't care less about the alibis. I was just being polite when I mentioned them. In fact, I've known who killed Red Edwards ever since you told me about the contents of his library and those five red circles. Frankly, I expected the five of *you* to come up with something more challenging."

Challenge to the Reader

Who did kill Red Edwards? And how did Ellery know?

THE SOLUTION

"All right, Mr. Smarty Pants," said little Emmy Wandermere, "which of the three suspects killed Big Red?"

"None of them," Ellery smiled. "You made a point of telling me that the dead man was a fan of Golden Age crime fiction. He circled four cheeses on his advertising flyer and numbered them one to four: Romano, Brie, Gouda, and feta, in that order. In other words, first a *Roman* cheese, second a *French* cheese, third a *Dutch* cheese, and fourth a *Greek* cheese."

"Damn and blast," said Dr. Vreeland, "he's done it again."

"It was obvious to me of all people," Ellery went on, "that the four circled cheeses were references to my first four novels in order of publication: *The Roman Hat Mystery, The French Powder Mystery, The Dutch Shoe Mystery,* and *The Greek Coffin Mystery.* The fifth circle was drawn around an area of white space, apparently because—ahem—there was no Roumi at the Inns, but it—"

"This is what got you an Edgar?" murmured Miss Wandermere.

"—but it was quite plainly meant to point to the title of my fifth book, *The Egyptian Cross Mystery.* I suggest the police check into the alibi of Mrs. Edwards' lover Achmed, the gardener from Cairo."

"Speaking of cheese," Syres said, as the door to the dining room swung open and Charles announced that dinner was served, "I believe Charlot is starting us off with a delectable Welsh rarebit."

"Allow me," said Ellery, taking Emmy Wandermere's arm. "If we hurry, we'll be just in time for the first course."

THE ADVENTURE OF THE BLACK-AND-BLUE CARBUNCLE

originally published in *Ellery Queen's Mystery Magazine* (November/December 2020)

INTRODUCTION BY KURT SERCU:

How exciting it would be to find it in my mailbox: an invitation, penned in some secret code on expensive card stock. At the top, where you might expect to see a name or other heading, nothing but a large golden question mark. An invitation to attend a meeting of the Puzzle Club—imagine that! To finally have the opportunity to meet that group of notables—including Ellery Queen himself—in the flesh!

Who hasn't dreamt of sipping a Scotch with Ellery and dining on Charlot's suprêmes de volaille aux huîtres, *with its hint of a reference to the Sherlock Holmes story whose title is punned upon in Pachter's pastiche, though in this case the carbuncle is a painful medical condition and not a gemstone....*

It's challenging for the writers of detective short stories to conceal many clues in their works, given the limited word-count they have to work with. *Obviously the investigator has to be given all of the keys necessary to unlock the mystery at hand. And fair play requires that everything needed to reach a solution must also be available to the reader—or, in the case of the Puzzle Club stories, to the occupant of the Problem Chair.*

No crime-fiction fan would deny those conventions of the form. And it's for exactly that reason that some critics of Ellery Queen's The Finishing Stroke *find it problematic that the solution to the novel's central crime requires the reader to be familiar with the Phoenician alphabet.*

This is the fine line crime writers must walk: the mystery has to be solvable by the reader, but the solution can't be too obvious. If every *reader could beat the detective to the solution, what need would we have for Ellery Queen?...*

Josh warned me that it might be impossible for me to beat Ellery to the solution of "The Adventure of the Black-and-Blue Carbuncle," since I'm not American born and bred. But I found myself focusing on a different question, rather than on the identity of the killer. In this story, you will meet an astronomer, Professor Lee Dannay. There's no physical description of the character, but as I read the story I felt that I could see him: a balding, bespectacled, bearded academic in a rumpled suit. Certainly a familiar image, and not unlike the way Frederic Dannay and Manfred B. Lee might have looked, had they been one person rather than a pair of cousins.

And, now that I think of it, perhaps just a bit like Josh himself looks, minus the suit....

The first two weeks of December had been unseasonably warm for New York, but it began to snow shortly past noon and, by the time Ellery Queen's Uber pulled up before the Park Avenue skyscraper that housed the aerie of Syres the multimillionaire, it was beginning to look a lot like Christmas.

To his surprise, the penthouse door was opened by bald, bearded Anatoly Arkavy, who was at seventy-two the youngest of the Puzzle Club's six members.

"Where's Charles?" asked Ellery, pronouncing it "Sharl", *a la Française*.

Arkavy took his unlit cigar out of his mouth and said, "In the kitchen."

Ellery's heart skipped a beat. "You mean Charlot is—?"

The biochemist clapped him on the shoulder. "He is at a funeral, Mr. Queen," he smiled, "but not his own, not yet. An old friend of his passed, and Charlot has gone back to France for the service. His son's in charge of the kitchen tonight, and that means I'm filling in as our butler *du jour*. Appropriately, there's turkey with all the trimmings on the menu." He noticed the white flakes melting on the shoulders of Ellery's trench coat. "Still snowing, is it?"

"A trenchant deduction," said Ellery, and the two of them

trooped down the hall, past Syres' astounding collection of French Impressionist art, to the study.

And there the rest of them were: Syres in his wheelchair, Darnell the renowned defense attorney, Vreeland the psychiatrist, and Pulitzer Prize-winning poetess Emmy Wandermere.

The Puzzle Club.

With Charles busy in the kitchen, Darnell had been deputized to man the bar, and he pressed a Scotch and soda into Ellery's hand and waved him to the overstuffed Chesterfield the club's members had christened the Problem Chair.

"Me again?" said Ellery, though he knew full well that it was. Otherwise, he would have been invited to the pre-meeting meeting, at which the five of them *not* destined for the Problem Chair would craft an enigma with which to challenge the "lucky" member whose turn it was to unravel the evening's riddle.

"It's a little after midnight at Mount Ramolap Observatory," Dr. Vreeland began, "and—"

"Mount Ramolap," said Ellery drily. "Which of you geniuses came up with that one?"

Little Emmy Wandermere put up a shy hand. "I thought it was clever."

"I'm not complaining," said Ellery. "Palomar spelled backwards. I like it."

The poetess looked relieved.

"As I say," Vreeland resumed, "it's midnight at the observatory, and Professor—oh, what the hell—Professor Lee Dannay is hunched over the controls of his radio telescope. Professor Dannay is a SETI researcher—"

"The Search for Extra-Terrestrial Intelligence," Ellery murmured.

"Correct, and night after night he listens in on one small sector of the galaxy, hoping for anything out of the ordinary, anything that might indicate we humans are not the only intelligent species in the universe."

"That implies that you consider *us* an intelligent species, then, Doctor?"

"I consider us—"

"That's another matter altogether, El," Syres the oilman broke in. "On the night in question, Professor Dannay is listening intently to the cosmos, when suddenly, to his astonishment, he hears something."

"Little Green Men from Space?" asked Ellery innocently.

"Not at all," croaked Syres. "What the professor hears are the footsteps of one Little White Man from Earth—or, actually, it would be better to say one Earthling, since size and color and gender can not be distinguished from the sound of these footsteps."

"Whoever it may be," Emmy Wandermere took up the tale, "it's someone who isn't supposed to be there, since only Professor Dannay is authorized to be in the building at this hour. 'Who's that?' he calls out, but there is no response. And then the intruder emerges from the shadows, and the professor's gaze is riveted by the double-action revolver held in his visitor's outstretched hand."

"The plot thickens," said Ellery.

"It does, indeed. The visitor gestures, waving the professor over to the writing desk in a corner of the observatory, and orders him to find a piece of paper and a pen."

"I was wondering when we'd get to the dying message," Ellery nodded.

"This isn't exactly a dying message," said Professor Arkavy in his heavy Russian accent, "although in a manner of speaking I suppose it is. As the professor crosses the tiled observatory floor, the person with the gun notices him hobbling and inquires as to the reason for his limp. 'I have a carbuncle on my big toe,' the professor replies, 'and, as if that's not enough of an impediment, I accidentally tripped over a footstool in my study last night, after I'd turned out the lights and was on my way up to bed, and my toe is now also black and blue.'"

"Is this relevant?" asked Ellery politely.

Darnell the attorney sipped at his martini. "At this stage of the game, Queen, *everything* is relevant."

Ellery set his own glass on the mahogany end table beside the Problem Chair, leaned back against the cushions, and folded his hands across his belly. "Proceed," he said.

"Once Dannay has paper and pen in hand," Darnell seamlessly picked up the tale, "his armed visitor orders him to write a suicide note. 'I have no intention of committing suicide,' the professor objects, to which his visitor responds by wordlessly cocking the pistol."

"According to Miss Wandermere," Ellery objected, "it was a revolver, not a pistol—and a double-action revolver, by the by, does not require cocking, since a single trigger pull will both cock the hammer and—"

"My dear boy," said the poetess, "would you kindly shut your trap and allow counsel for the offense to get on with the story?"

"I was just—"

"You were *in*just," Darnell cut him off. "And for the purposes of this puzzle, truly, whether it's a pistol or a revolver doesn't matter. It is a *gun*, and the visitor *cocks* it. Is that all right with you?"

Ellery pursed his lips. "Perfectly," he nodded. "Carry on."

"I'll take it from here," said Syres from his wheelchair. "The visitor with the gun orders Dannay to write a suicide note, El, and warns him not to try any tricks. Dannay thinks for a moment and writes: 'Many very educated men would say that suicide is the coward's way out. I don't consider myself to be a coward, but....' He carries on writing for a few minutes longer, and finally signs the note 'Dannay, comma, Lee' with a broad flourish."

"At which point," Dr. Vreeland concluded, "the trigger of the double-action revolver is pulled, which both cocks the hammer and releases it, firing a single .38 Special round through and through the professor's brain, killing him instantly."

There was a long silence in the room as the imaginary echo of the shot faded. Then Ellery raised his glass and toasted Professor Lee Dannay's memory and took a healthy swallow of Scotch.

"There are, I take it, the usual three suspects?" he said.

"Of course there are," said Emmy Wandermere. "Aren't there always?"*

**Actually, not* always. *See "A Study in* Scarlett!"

"The prime suspect," said Darnell, "is Gilbert Theodore Knott, a graduate student at the university. For the last six months, he's been doing research for a paper Professor Dannay recently submitted to *The Astronomical Journal*—and the professor neither listed him as a co-author nor thanked him in the paper's acknowledgments."

"Second," said Professor Arkavy, "is Dannay's colleague, Associate Professor Roy Astor, who has repeatedly requested an increase in his allotted telescope time, a request Professor Dannay, his superior in the observatory's hierarchy, has repeatedly refused to grant."

"And finally," Emmy Wandermere chimed in, "we introduce the woman in the case: auburn-haired Catherine Dannay, *née* Catherine Haring, the professor's wife, who has long suspected—incorrectly, as it turns out—her husband of having an affair with another of his grad students, a comely co-ed whose name is, I assure you, dear boy, of no importance whatsoever to our puzzle."

"And there you have it, Mr. Queen," said Professor Arkavy. "You may now have the usual one hour to ask questions."

"I do have two questions," Ellery said, sipping scotch. "First, did the professor normally sign himself last-name-comma-first-name? That's an unusual practice for a signature."

"Seriously?" growled Darnell. "That's your *first* question?"

"Hold on, Clarence Darrow," Emmy Wandermere cautioned, laying a wrinkled hand on the attorney's sleeve. "Let's hear the man out before we kill ourselves."

"My second question is rhetorical," Ellery went on remorselessly. "Didn't you once promise me you wouldn't repeat a gimmick from one of our previous puzzles in any of the subsequent ones?"

"We did," acknowledged Dr. Vreeland.*

"Then how do you explain—?"

**Again, see "A Study in* Scarlett*!"*

"We changed our minds," said Emmy Wandermere sheepishly. "And *now* I believe we can go ahead and kill ourselves."

"Damn and blast," sighed Syres, the multimillionaire, "the man's done it again!"

Challenge to the Reader

Who killed Lee Dannay? And how did Ellery know?

THE SOLUTION

"Mount Ramolap was your first hint," Ellery explained. "I admired the cleverness of the backwards spelling of Mount Palomar when you originally mentioned it, Dr. Vreeland, but I didn't realize until later that it was in fact a subtle clue to the solution of the puzzle."

"What put you on the right track, then?" asked Professor Arkavy.

"The suicide note, of course," Emmy Wandermere scowled.

"Of course," said Ellery. "In the puzzle I wrote up as 'The Three Students,'* the clue that gave the game away was a folded slip of paper on which was printed, in unidentifiable block lettering, the apparently nonsensical rhyme"—he cleared his throat—"'On old Olympus' towering top / A Finn and German viewed a hop.'"

"A Finn and a German?" repeated Anatoly Arkavy, shaking his bald head in bewilderment.

"You were off on one of your infernal—that is to say *eternal*—lecture tours," Miss Wandermere told him, "so you missed that meeting. Our resident shrink came up with the puzzle, which was based on a memory aid medical students use to remember the names of the twelve cranial nerves."

"I was positive it would stump our resident sleuth," Dr. Vreeland admitted. "Why in the *world* would a mystery writer be familiar with that esoteric mnemonic device?"

"I *warned* you," the poetess said. "The man knows *everything*, and he never forgets any of it, no matter how useless. He's told us that himself."

"May I continue?" asked Ellery politely. When no one objected, he went on: "Ordered to compose a suicide note, your Professor Dannay wrote, 'Many very educated men would say that suicide is the coward's way out.' The beginning of that sentence struck a chord with me: I recognized it as the opening words to

*see "*The Three Students*"

yet another mnemonic—'Many Very Educated Men Are Just Silly Under Normal Pressure'—which young stargazers use to remember the order of the planets outward from the sun, including the location of the asteroid belt: *Many* is Mercury, *Very* is Venus, *Educated* is Earth, and so on."

"I *warned* you," Miss Wandermere said again, raising her glass of chardonnay to her lips with both hands. "It's never a good idea to drink twice from the same well."

"Professor Dannay veered away from the mnemonic after 'men,' though," Ellery resumed, "which drew my attention to its next word, the first word he didn't use in his suicide note, the word 'Are,' which is there to remind middle-schoolers that the asteroid belt is found between Mars and Jupiter."

Ellery drained the last of his drink.

"But why, I wondered, did our doomed astronomer sign his name backwards? I tried similarly reversing the names of the three suspects and saw at once that Gilbert Theodore Knott—abbreviated as Gil T. Knott—was in fact 'not guilty.'"

"Well, what about Catherine Dannay?" demanded old Syres. "Reverse *her* name and you get what? Dannay, Cathy? How does that help you?"

"You mean Catherine *Haring* Dannay," Ellery grinned, "she of the auburn hair? Obviously, Mine Host, the professor's wife was nothing but a 'Red' Haring."

Darnell the attorney ground his teeth. "Damn you, Queen," he said. "You take all the fun out of this."

"Which leaves only Associate Professor Roy Astor," Ellery smiled. "Whose name, when reversed, is 'Astor, Roy,' and whose repeatedly frustrated desire for more telescope time was his motive for murder."

Ellery rose from the Puzzle Chair and helped little Emmy Wandermere to her feet.

"Speaking of asteroids," Ellery said, holding up his empty highball glass to Darnell the bartender, "I could use another belt. And if you will have the goodness to touch the bell, Dr. Vreeland, we will begin another investigation, in which a bird will be the chief feature."

THE FIVE ORANGE PIPES

originally published in *Ellery Queen's Mystery Magazine* (January/February 2021)

INTRODUCTION BY JON L. BREEN:

Early in "The Five Orange Pipes," it is noted that the Puzzle Club is back in business after about a half century between meetings. I'm the sort of person who always does the math: if so-and-so is that age in that year, then he must be this age in this year. That usually works for real people, but it gets tricky when you apply it to fictional characters. The Finishing Stroke *(1958) clearly states that Ellery Queen the character was born in 1905, not coincidentally the birth year of his two creators, Frederic Dannay and Manfred B. Lee. The main action of the book takes place around Christmas 1929, the year young Ellery's first novel,* The Roman Hat Mystery, *was published, and the final section flashes forward to 1957, at which time Ellery finally solves the case that had haunted him over the years.*

Based on that timeline, Ellery would at the time of "The Five Orange Pipes" be a hundred and fifteen years old or thereabouts. If that bothers you, it shouldn't. Non-aging fictional characters are traditional, especially in detective stories. Take, for example, Nero Wolfe and Archie Goodwin, who are about the same ages from 1934 to 1975, while history goes by around them. Even characters who seem to get older from book to book—Rebus, say, or Harry Bosch—age more slowly than they would in real time.

The fact is that there are at least three separate timelines in the Queen saga. Ignore the foreword to The Roman Hat Mystery, *attributed to one J. J. McC., which claims that Ellery and his father have moved to Italy and that Ellery has a wife and child—who are never mentioned again. Obviously pure codswallop. The contemporary references in that first novel are appropriate to the 1920s ("... in the dramatic season of 192- Eugene O'Neill had neglected to write a new play" and patrons "had deserted the legitimate theatre for the more ingenuous delights of the motion-picture palaces") and those in the last novel,* A Fine and Private Place *(1971), are appropriate to the 1960s, but Ellery remains a young man. When Edward D. Hoch and I were asked by EQMM editor Janet Hutchings to do pastiches to celebrate* Roman Hat's *seventieth anniversary in the late 1990s, we both followed that non-aging policy; I had no desire to disorient my fellow math-doers by making reference to rap music and Y2K in my story. Dale Andrews, on the other hand, has written about a senior-citizen Ellery in several pastiches.*

In addition to real time and fantasy fictional time, there is a third timeline to consider: Inspector Richard Queen, Ellery's father, retires from the NYPD in Inspector Queen's Own Case *(1956), and in* The House of Brass *(1968) he's still retired. But in several books written between or after those two, he remains on the job.*

I recommend that you don't worry about how old anybody is and just enjoy the puzzles Josh Pachter has presented. The one that follows is a doozy.

For all the years of the Puzzle Club's existence—and the club's existence stretched back half a century by now, though it had been inactive for several decades before its resurrection in 2019—there was an unwritten rule that all food and drink would be provided by its regular host, Cyrus Syres, who had made his millions in the Texas oilfields and retired to a New York penthouse to live out the rest of his days in the Big Apple.

It was, therefore, unusual to see Ellery Queen step out of the Uber he now preferred to the traditional Yellow Cab carrying a large Morton Williams bag in his arms, and when Charles—pronounced "Sharl", *a la Française*—opened the penthouse door to his ring, a quizzical look flitted across the butler's normally stoic countenance at the unexpected sight.

"May I take that for you, sir?" he asked deferentially. "Shall I bring it back to Charlot in the kitchen?"

"No, thanks," said Ellery. "I'm sure your father doesn't need any shopping assistance from me—though, from what I can smell from here, he *has* taken my suggestion about tonight's menu. I anticipate a superb meal when the business portion of our meeting has been concluded. Anyway, these aren't groceries. They're gifts for the membership, and I'll carry them back myself."

He followed Charles down the long hallway—admiring as always the Manets and Monets and Renoirs and Gauguins that lined its walls, along with a delightful Van Gogh pencil sketch he couldn't remember having seen before—to the study, where Syres and the four other members of the club awaited his arrival.

"This is highly irregular, Queen," Darnell, the defense attorney, greeted him, martini in hand. "You know full well that our procedure is for five of us to gather early to invent a puzzle for our sixth member to tackle, but tonight, per your instructions, we've done no preplanning whatsoever."

"Yes, dear boy, what's the big idea?" said Emmy Wandermere, the Pulitzer Prize-winning poet, irrepressible as always.

Ellery sank into the overstuffed Chesterfield the six of them affectionately called the Problem Chair, his bag on his lap, his arms wrapped protectively around it. Charles handed him his customary highball, and he took a grateful sip.

"It's time to take the cat out of that bag, Mr. Queen," said the bald and bearded Anatoly Arkavy, whose imperfect command of English-language idioms betrayed his Russian upbringing.

"Not a cat," said Ellery with a curious smile, "but a cap. *Five* caps, to be precise. Plus five orange pipes." And he reached into his paper sack and began pulling forth and distributing checkered deerstalkers and ornately hand-carved pipes, one of each to Miss Wandermere, Darnell, Professor Arkavy, Dr. Vreeland the psychiatrist, and Syres, their host.

"It may have escaped your notice," he went on, "but tonight is the anniversary of our very first meeting—the fifty-sixth anniversary, to be exact—and I thought perhaps we might do something a little different to celebrate. Rather than five of us ganging up on one, as usual, I've worked out a little puzzle of my own for this evening, and the five of you get to play Sherlock Holmes."

"Thus," Vreeland observed, "the paraphernalia." He set his deerstalker at a rakish angle on his balding head, stuck his pipe in his mouth, and said "Elementary, my dear Queen" in a terrible attempt at a British accent, his *r*'s unmistakably American.

"Are these meerschaum?" asked Syres, examining the bowl of his own pipe.

"Alas, no," said Ellery. "Nat Sherman's was fresh out of sepiolite. These are—"

"Sepio*what?*" asked Emmy Wandermere, peering up from beneath the brim of her hat.

"Sepiolite," said Professor Arkavy, who had been before his retirement one of the world's leading biochemists. "A complex magnesium silicate—or, in layman's terms, a soft white clay mineral often used in the manufacture of pipes for smoking."

"It's a common misconception that Holmes preferred a meerschaum or a calabash," Ellery explained. "In the original novels and short stories, he's described as smoking briar pipes, clay pipes, and sometimes cherrywood pipes, but Conan Doyle never provided a great deal of detail. These, in any case, were carved from orangewood, and they were, I thought, the most authentically Sherlockian items in the shop."

"I've never been quite sure," said Dr. Vreeland, "if 'Sherlockian' or 'Holmesian' is the proper term."

Ellery coughed academically into his fist. "Allow me to enlighten you. Although the words are equivalent in meaning, we tend to use 'Sherlockian' in the United States, while our British friends across the pond say 'Holmesian.'"

"So we're to play Sherlock this evening," Darnell summed up, "while you will take the role of—who? Surely not Dr. Watson, that stumbling, bumbling—"

"Another myth," Ellery cut him off, "originated and perpetuated by the endearing but completely non-Canonical performance of Nigel Bruce in the Basil Rathbone films. In the original texts, Watson was in fact quite intelligent—in no way Holmes' equal, of course, but certainly not a fool. I hadn't really thought of myself as playing a part tonight, but, yes, let me be Dr. John H. Watson, late of the Fifth Northumberland Fusiliers and subsequently the Sixty-sixth (Berkshire) Regiment of Foot."

"Oh, stop showing off your vast storehouse of trivia, dear boy," said Emmy Wandermere, "and get *on* with it!"

"As you wish," said Ellery. "So, speaking of performers who

have tackled the role of the Great Detective of Baker Street, we begin tonight's tale with—I'm going to call him Brett Jeremy, star of stage and screen, who returns home from the Monday-night performance of his acclaimed Broadway revival of William Gillette's *Sherlock Holmes,* only to—"

"Hold it right there, Mr. Queen," Dr. Vreeland butted in. "Broadway theaters are dark on Mondays."

"In the real world, certainly. But this is *my* story, and *my* Broadway theaters are open when I *tell* them to be open. So, with your permission?"

The psychiatrist waved a gracious hand.

"Brett Jeremy returns from *his* Broadway theater, only to—"

Now it was Syres turn to interrupt. "The Sherbert on West Forty-Seventh Street, no doubt?"*

"Do you want to hear the puzzle, Cyrus, or not?"

"Sorry, El. Do go on."

"As I have been *trying* to say, Brett Jeremy returns from his Monday-evening performance at the famous *Shubert* Theater on West *44th* Street, only to find that his, shall we say, 'companion' Henry is missing from the apartment they share on West 87th. Robert and, ahem, Ellery—who have been visiting with them for the last couple of days—are lying on the living-room floor, dead. There is a pitcher of water on the coffee table that sits in front of the sofa, and also a single water glass. There is shattered glass on the parquet floor beside the bodies, and the hardwood itself is wet. The large window looking out onto Eighty-seventh Street is wide open."

He paused and took a sip of his Scotch and water.

"And?" asked Anatoly Arkavy.

"And that's it," said Ellery.

"That's *it?*" echoed little Emmy Wandermere. "Then what's the puzzle? Obviously Henry killed them and fled."

"Correct," Ellery nodded. "But the puzzle is this: what was the proximate *cause* of Robert's and Ellery's deaths? You may, as usual, have one hour to interrogate your interlocutor."

*see "*A Study in* Scarlett!"

The room exploded.

"Did Robert and Ellery also live in the apartment?" said Professor Arkavy, beginning the questioning.

"Already answered," Ellery tut-tutted. "They were visitors, had been there for several days and were originally going to remain for the rest of the week."

"Were they brothers?"

"They were not."

"Were they related in any way?"

"No."

"Friends, El?"

"I think it would acceptable to say that they were."

"Was either of them an actor?"

"No."

"Was either of them romantically involved with Brett Jeremy?"

"No."

"With Henry?"

"No again: romance does not enter into the picture here."

"Were they both killed in the same way?"

"They were."

"Were they shot?"

"No."

"Stabbed?"

"No."

"Poisoned?"

"Well, not really, no."

"Strangled?"

"Again, not really."

There was a lull, filled by Charles, who walked around the study with a tray, collecting empty glasses and replacing them with a new round of fortifying beverages.

Dr. Vreeland took a healthy slug of bourbon and said, "They weren't killed by ice arrows fired through the open window, were they, and—?"

"—and then the arrows melted," suggested Syres eagerly,

"which accounts for the wet floor!"

"But not the broken glass," Darnell objected. "And besides, he's already told us they weren't shot."

"Not by a bullet, no, but—"

"Bullet or arrow," said Professor Arkavy, waggling his unlit cigar like a classroom pointer, "shot is shot, and they *weren't* shot."

"No shot, Sherlock," murmured Emmy Wandermere, adjusting her deerstalker and pretending to take a puff of her orange pipe.

"Then how on Earth did they die?" growled Vreeland, frustrated.

"Ay," said Ellery, stroking his chin mysteriously, "there's the rub."

"Blunt trauma?" Anatoly Arkavy proposed.

"Professor Plum did it," Miss Wandermere piped up. "He coshed them with the candlestick. In the conservatory."

"No, *Henry* did it," Ellery reminded them. "And he didn't cosh them, in the head or any other part of their anatomy." His silver-gray eyes glittered. "And Brett Jeremy and Henry lived in a two-bedroom apartment. No conservatory, no billiard room, no lounge or study."

"The kitchen?" the poetess tried.

"The living room," Ellery said firmly. "If you're looking for a clue to this game, Emmy, you won't find it in the game of Clue."

The questioning resumed. But the allotted hour passed quickly, and at the end of it Syres, Arkady, Vreeland, Darnell, and little Miss Wandermere were forced to admit defeat.

"All right, El," Syres croaked, "how did Robert and Ellery die? Spill it."

"Ah, interesting," Ellery grinned. "In a way, that's the most important thing anyone's said all evening."

Challenge to the Reader

How did *Robert and, ahem, Ellery die?*

THE SOLUTION

"Forty-some years ago," Ellery said, "I was watching the television version of *The Odd Couple,* and I've never forgotten something Tony Randall said as Felix Unger in an episode titled, if memory serves, 'My Strife in Court.' Felix and Oscar are arrested for scalping tickets to a Broadway show—not, I should add, *Sherlock Holmes*—and Felix decides to represent them. A witness for the prosecution testifies that she's assumed something—it doesn't matter what—and Felix chalks the word 'assume' on a blackboard and triumphantly says, 'You should never assume. Because, when you *assume,* you make an *ass* of *u* and *me.*' You quoted that line yourself, Emmy, the first time our club regathered after its long hiatus.* But the five of you made a significant assumption as you listened to my story."

Emmy Wandermere leaned closer to Professor Arkavy and stage-whispered, "Is he calling us asses?"

"Shh," the Russian told her. "Let the man have his fun."

"Your assumption," Ellery said, "was actually *two* assumptions rolled into one. For starters, you assumed that Henry must be either Brett Jeremy's flat mate, occupying the apartment's second bedroom, or his boyfriend. In fact, Henry *does* sleep in Brett's room—not in his bed, but in a basket *beside* his bed. Because Henry, you see, is—"

"*Desk Set!*" exclaimed Miss Wandermere.

"Henry is a desk set?" said Professor Arkavy, eyes narrowed.

"Not *a* desk set." Emmy shook her head in impatience. "The movie *Desk Set,* from the Fifties. There's a brief dialogue scene that uses a very similar puzzle."

Ellery nodded. "And if it was good enough for Tracy and Hepburn," he said, "I decided it would be good enough for the Puzzle Club. Spencer Tracy's character even gives Katharine Hepburn's a hint."

"Never assume," Emmy Wandermere sighed.

**Again, see "A Study in* Scarlett!"

"Exactly."

"So then," Dr. Vreeland mused, "Henry must be—"

"—a *cat!*" burst out Darnell the defense attorney.

"A particularly handsome Siamese," Ellery confirmed. "And Robert and Ellery aren't human, either—that was your second assumption. They're fish, and Brett Jeremy was pet-sitting them while their owner was away on a weeklong vacation. Brett was unused to taking care of any critters other than Henry, though, and he made the costly mistake of leaving their bowl on the coffee table in the living room. Henry, a curious cat—"

"Curiosity *killed* the cat," said Dr. Vreeland.

Ellery shook his head. "Not in this case. Robert and Ellery were swimming happily in their bowl, and Henry, curious about these strange newcomers to his household, swiped a paw at the bowl and knocked it to the hardwood floor, where it shattered. This terrified poor Henry, who leapt out the open window and padded down the fire escape to a lower floor, from which his master's voice later summoned him. So, in this case, curiosity killed the *fish*—which died of asphyxiation amidst the broken glass of their bowl on Brett Jeremy's drenched living-room floor."

Professor Arkavy muttered something in Russian that the rest of them recognized as an oath.

"Why didn't Henry *eat* the fish?" objected Miss Wandermere.

Ellery blinked, for once at a loss for an answer.

"Oh, Emmy, it's a *story*," Cyrus Syres grumbled. "If El's Broadway theater can be open on a Monday, that darned cat can certainly be frightened enough to flee from the scene of his crime without stopping for a snack."

Miss Wandermere subsided, mollified.

"But why in the world," said Darnell, "did you name one of the fish Ellery, Queen?"

Ellery smiled. "Because he was a particular *kind* of fish: a danio. And, in fact, a particular *breed* of danio: a—ahem—a *Queen* danio."

The attorney groaned. "And Robert? What kind of fish was he?"

"Actually," Ellery admitted, "*his* name has nothing to do with his breed. I named him after a very dear friend of mine, a crime writer who published a series of wonderful Sherlockian parodies in my magazine in the Sixties and Seventies, featuring a detective named Schlock Homes."

He paused expectantly, and Dr. Vreeland asked the question he was waiting for: "Your friend's name, Mr. Queen? Out with it!"

"My friend's name," Ellery said, "was Robert L.—"

"—*Fish*!" crowed the elderly oilman. "I spent a delightful half-hour with Bob Fish once, at a PEN meeting in the early Eighties, not long before he died."

"He was a delightful man," Ellery nodded, "and a marvelous writer."

"I can't remember," Syres went on, "if it was Bob Fish or Bob Bloch who said, 'Despite my ghoulish reputation, I have the heart of a small boy. I keep it in a jar on my desk.'"

"I've heard that line attributed to yet another author," Darnell mused.

"No disrespect to the very talented Mr. King," said Mr. Queen, "but I heard Robert Bloch—another great friend, and another great writer—say that classic line at a Mystery Writers of America cocktail party half a dozen years before Stephen King (or Richard Bachman, for that matter) first broke into print. I miss both Bobs very much."

In the silence that followed, Charles re-entered the study and cleared his throat. "Dinner is served," he announced. "My father hopes you'll enjoy the trout almondine he's prepared for you."

"Trout almondine," Emmy Wandermere repeated, setting her deerstalker more firmly atop her steel-gray curls. "I just *knew* there was something fishy about this whole evening."

And, for once, no one disagreed with her.

THEIR LAST BOW

originally published in *Ellery Queen's Mystery Magazine* (January/February 2022)

INTRODUCTION BY DALE C. ANDREWS:

As readers will see, "Their Last Bow" definitively ends the Puzzle Club mysteries. Introducing it provides me with an opportunity not only to reflect on the story itself, but also on the Puzzle Club series, begun by Dannay and Lee and now, over fifty years later, finally concluded here by Josh Pachter.

As the introduction to this volume points out, the Puzzle Club stories began very late in the arc of Ellery Queen mysteries—and the original series ended abruptly when, on April 3, 1971, Manfred Lee, the scribe of the EQ partnership, died of a heart attack on the dressing room floor of his Connecticut home.

The first five stories in this collection—those crafted by Dannay and Lee—were therefore the last examples we have of Ellery the detective as envisioned by the writers who created and nurtured him. And that Ellery is very different from the young dandy we first met in The Roman Hat Mystery *in 1929.*

Much has been written about the evolution of the Ellery Queen character. During his literary life—spanning the period from 1929 to 1970—he changed from a callow, foppish pedagogue to a more empathetic and realistic individual. But the Ellery Queen mysteries share a simple formula: murder cloaked in a puzzle. The early Queen novels, from Roman Hat *through* Halfway House, *tend to accentuate the puzzle aspect, allowing a detached Ellery to sidestep the very human reactions that in real life would accompany his involvement in the investigation of a violent death. But Dannay and Lee changed course in the second half of the Queen oeuvre. From* Halfway House *on, we see a different Ellery—less removed, more involved, more questioning of his own abilities, more willing to confront and empathize with the plight of victims and their survivors.*

Humanizing Ellery improved the literary value of the Queen mysteries. But this did not come easily, and it proved particularly difficult for Lee, who was tasked with bringing to life Dannay's outlines. Joseph Goodrich, in Blood Relations, *quotes the following from a letter Lee sent to Dannay in 1950:*

> *Within the demands of necessity, you have carefully, sometimes brilliantly worked out what must follow. While recognizing, even applauding all this, I still look at the result and I must say, "But how fantastic. Who would—could—do such a thing?" Nobody human. It doesn't ring true to life in exactly ... the proportion it was brilliantly conceived. The more brilliant, the less true, the less convincing. Yet I have to write this story in terms of people in a recognizable "realistic" background.*

What was likely the most difficult for the cousins in all of this was the need to realistically portray the violence and death that were the linchpins of the EQ mysteries. In many ways, this task ran contrary to the best natures of Dannay and Lee. As the New York Times *noted, in its 1971 obituary of Lee:*

> *Both writers detested violence and never owned guns or went hunting. Indeed, force is almost always an inconsequential factor in their books, heavily outweighed by the brilliant deductions of Ellery Queen or the fantastic machinations of his antagonists.*

Why delve into all of this in introducing "Their Last Bow"? Well, put simply, it has always seemed to me that the Puzzle Club stories afforded a sanctuary for the cousins at the end of their writing careers from the reality of dealing with death. Within the protected environment of the Puzzle Club, Dannay and Lee fashioned an approach that allowed the puzzle to once again reign supreme. Ellery can realistically be portrayed—while death and its attendant sorrows can once again be neatly sidestepped. The reader—like Ellery—knows from the outset of each story that the puzzle is an artifice. It is wholly concocted, premised on a death that is not, in fact, real.

All of this is why I like "Their Last Bow" so much. Josh ends the Puzzle Club series by breaking this mold, and in doing so reminds us that, all too often—and all cleverness aside—the piper must ultimately be paid. The reality of death can sometimes be finessed, but it will eventually intrude and must be confronted, as is the case here.

At the same time Ellery—like Sherlock Holmes before him—must also confront a larger reality: the fact that, in the midst of complacency, the world will often pull the rug out from under us. "Their Last Bow" was written in 2020, a year that taught all of us that lesson.

Inspector Richard Queen, dressed head to toe as Santa Claus in jolly red suit and tasseled cap and long white beard, stood beside an enormous black Salvation Army kettle. With a merry twinkle in his eyes, his little round belly shaking when he laughed (like, yes, *exactly* like a bowl full of jelly), he rang a huge golden bell, again and again and again, the tintinnabulation echoing louder and louder until—

Ellery opened his eyes and groaned. He groped for his bifocals on the nightstand beside his bed, put them on, and picked up his ringing landline. According to the illuminated numerals on his alarm clock, it was 2:13 A.M.

"Monsieur Queen?" a quavering voice asked. "Is that you?"

"Do you know what time it—who in the name of God are *you*?" he demanded blearily.

"*Mes excuses*," the voice said. "I am so sorry to awaken you, m'sieur. It is I, Charlot."

"Charlot?" Ellery sat bolt upright, instantly awake. "What is it, *mon ami*? Mr. Syres?"

"I'm afraid so." The voice trembled with grief. "Please, Monsieur Queen, can you come at once?"

"Of course," Ellery said. "I'll be there *tout de suite*."

He banged down the phone, then snatched up his cell and ordered an Uber.

As the black Prius pulled up before the familiar apartment building on Park Avenue, Ellery saw Darnell, the notorious criminal attorney, nod abstractedly at the doorman and hurry across the tiled lobby to the elevator.

Ellery thanked his driver and, his body creaking, eased himself out of the passenger seat. The car pulled away from the curb, and an almost identical vehicle swung in to take its place. Little Emmy Wandermere, the Pulitzer Prize-winning poet, jumped out, her gray hair still tousled with sleep.

"Charlot called you?" she yipped.

Ellery nodded. "Darnell's just gone in. Come on!"

They had to wait two long minutes for the elevator to return to the lobby and rode up in tense silence. The penthouse door was flung open by a frantic Charlot, who raced down the corridor past Syres' marvelous collection of Impressionist paintings to the study, the two of them scurrying in his wake.

Darnell was shrugging out of his overcoat, and the other members of the Puzzle Club—the two doctors, Vreeland and Arkavy—were bent over the shriveled figure of Cyrus Syres, their old friend and founder of the club, who sat motionless in the wheelchair to which he had been confined for the last twenty years.

"Is he—?" gasped Miss Wandermere, grabbing Ellery's hand in fear.

Anatoly Arkavy looked up from the body. "I'm afraid so," he said, in his thick Russian accent.

"Was he—?" asked Ellery, squeezing the poet's hand tightly.

"—murdered?" said Dr. Vreeland. "I'm a psychiatrist, Mr. Queen, not a forensic pathologist."

"And I'm a chemist," added Professor Arkavy. "How should we know?"

"Isn't that question more in *your* line, Queen?" said Darnell.

"I suppose it is," said Ellery. He turned to Charlot. "You found him like this?"

The old chef nodded. "I came in to say good night, and 'e was—like this, yes. I felt for a pulse, but there was nothing. So I called the doctors first, and then the rest of you."

Ellery waved the rest of them off and studied the scene. Syres' wheelchair was pulled up before a wheeled wooden taboret he recognized from the Puzzle Club's meetings, at which it had since the club's founding many years ago served as an impromptu bar. Tonight, though, it had apparently been used for a game of solitaire. A deck of cards had been laid out in the traditional Patience format: a tableau of seven columns in various stages of play, four foundation piles with the four aces at their bottoms, a stock pile and a waste pile. Poor Syres held a single card face down in his lifeless right hand, the classic blue bicyclists gazing up blankly from beneath his stubby thumb.

Lying flat on the four corners of the little table were four magazines: the current issue of *Poetry* and recent numbers of *The Biochemist, ABA Journal,* and *Psychology Today*.

"I have a villanelle in this month's *Poetry*," said Emmy Wandermere.

"I coauthored a research paper that's abstracted in that issue of *The Biochemist*," said Professor Arkavy.

"There's an editorial of mine on mandatory minimum sentencing in the American Bar Association's journal," said Darnell.

"And my last book was reviewed in the new *Psych Today*," said Dr. Vreeland.

The four of them turned to Ellery.

"No *Ellery Queen's Mystery Magazine*, dear boy," said Emmy Wandermere slowly. "I have to ask myself: why not?"

"Isn't the idea of a *missing* clue a sort of trademark of yours, Mr. Queen?" Dr. Vreeland wondered aloud.

"It certainly is," Ellery agreed, "going all the way back to the missing top hat in my very first book, *The Roman Hat Mystery*." He leaned over the body and reached for Syres' hand.

"You shouldn't touch anything," cautioned Darnell. "You know that, Queen."

"I do," Ellery confirmed. And he gently took hold of the multimillionaire's hand and turned it over, revealing the face of the card the dead man was holding.

It was the Queen of Clubs.

"The Queen," he said aloud.

"The Queen of *Clubs,*" added Professor Arkavy, looking quizzically around the study at the surviving members of the Puzzle Club.

"That's interesting," Dr. Vreeland observed. "Why did he select that particular card?"

"A dying message?" mused Darnell. "That's another of your tropes, Queen, am I right?"

Ellery pursed his lips and nodded.

"He seems to have named you, Mr. Queen," Professor Arkavy said. "Or was he simply drawing our attention to the nonspecific idea of an honor card—ace, king, queen, jack, ten?"

"Perhaps," Darnell suggested, "it's the suit that's important? Or the color?"

"What's *wrong* with you people?" cried little Miss Wandermere. "This isn't one of our silly pre-dinner puzzles. Charles"—she pronounced it "Sharl", *a la Française*—"isn't mixing cocktails. Charlot hasn't got dinner waiting for us. I'm not going to stand here and let you treat Cyrus's death like some kind of parlor game!"

"Emmy is right," said Arkavy. "If someone killed our friend Syres, this is a job for the professionals. We should notify the proper authorities."

"Shall I place the call?" asked Charlot, unwilling to make such a momentous decision on his own.

"Not quite yet," said Ellery. "Before you do, perhaps I should explain what happened here tonight."

The words ricocheted around the room like the crack of a gunshot.

"You *know?*" asked Emmy Wandermere breathlessly. "Was he murdered, dear boy? By one of us?"

"Out with it, Queen," commanded Darnell. "Which of us killed him, and for God sakes, *why?*"

"None of us killed him," Ellery announced. "I disagree with

Anatoly, Emmy: when you say this isn't a parlor game, I think you're wrong. Cyrus was old, and ill, and perhaps not thinking as clearly as he once did. He knew he was at the very end of his life, and he saw his impending passing as an opportunity to present the five of us with one final problem. So he gathered together those magazines and laid out a game of solitaire, made sure he had the Queen of Clubs in his hand, and then he simply sat there in his wheelchair, waiting to die, relishing the riddle he was leaving behind for us to solve."

"*Not* a murder, then," said Dr. Vreeland solemnly. "Not a crime."

"All the same," Darnell told them, "we'll have to call it in. Charlot?"

The old chef picked up the phone and punched out 9-1-1.

"I suppose this is the end of the line for us," said Professor Arkavy. "I can't imagine the Puzzle Club continuing without our longtime host."

"The end of the line," Dr. Vreeland echoed.

"And the rest," intoned Emmy Wandermere, ever the poet, "is silence."

Three hours later, after the police had been and gone and the Medical Examiner's team had taken away the body and the rest of them had gone home and back to bed, Ellery and Charlot rode down in the elevator together.

They avoided each other's gaze. Instead, they stood shoulder to shoulder in the descending car, facing forward, each studying the illuminated floor numbers above the door.

When the indicator reached "14," Ellery finally spoke.

"I know the truth," he said.

"The truth?" said Charlot.

"I know who killed Mr. Syres."

Charlot's tired eyes narrowed. "You mean 'e *was* murdered, after all?"

"He was."

"Then tell me, Monsieur Queen," the old man pleaded, "'oo killed 'im?"

Challenge to the Reader

Who did kill *Cyrus Syres? And how did Ellery know?*

THE SOLUTION

"*You* killed him," Ellery said.

The silence that followed was thick enough to carve with one of Charlot's Laguiole knives.

The old man looked down from the numbers and studied Ellery for a long moment.

Then he nodded his head.

"'e was in pain," he said simply. "'e knew the end was near, but 'e couldn't wait any longer. 'e asked me to 'elp 'im, and I did. 'ow did you know it was me?"

"There was no giveaway clue," Ellery said, "no dying message to interpret, no mystery to unravel, no brilliant deduction based on logic and ratiocination. In the real world, Charlot, a detective sometimes simply *guesses* ... and, sometimes, he guesses right."

"There must 'ave been *something*," the Frenchman protested. "Some 'int that put you on the right track?"

"Well, the timing of your phone call, I suppose," said Ellery. "You worked for Mr. Syres on Puzzle Club nights, and for all I know on other special occasions as well. But there was no reason for you to be here at two in the morning tonight, a night when he wasn't entertaining guests. Unless there *was* a reason, after all—and what other reason could there have been?"

Charlot nodded somberly.

"But what about the magazines?" Ellery wondered. "The game of solitaire? The Queen of Clubs?"

""The game was real," the old man explained. "After I gave 'im the pills, 'e dealt out a hand of solitaire to pass the time while 'e waited for death to claim 'im. 'e was in the middle of the game when 'e—when 'e died. It was pure coincidence that the Queen of Clubs was in 'is hand at 'is final moment. But that's what gave me the idea. 'e 'as always followed all of your careers closely. I took down the magazines from 'is bookshelves, then made the calls. Monsieur Syres, 'e would have liked the idea of leaving you all with one final puzzle."

"I agree," Ellery said. "He would have liked that idea very much." He hesitated. "But why not a copy of *my* magazine,

EQMM?"

Charlot licked his lips. "The playing card was already there. I didn't see any reason to add another clue pointing in your direction."

Ellery pondered that for a moment, then shook his head. "There's something you're not telling me, Charlot."

The old man looked sheepish. "'e didn't like reading fiction," he whispered. "So 'e never bought your books—or your magazine."

Ellery parted with a rueful smile. "*Chacun à son goût*," he said.

"To each 'is own," the chef translated, as the elevator eased to a stop in the lobby.

The doorman swung the building's heavy glass door open for them, and they walked, side by side, out into the night.

Ellery turned up his collar. "There's an east wind coming, Charlot," he said.

"I think not, Monsieur Queen. It is very warm."

Ellery smiled, and paraphrased Sir Arthur Conan Doyle from memory: "Good old Charlot! You are the one fixed point in a changing age. There's an east wind coming all the same, such a wind as never blew on New York yet. It will be cold and bitter, Charlot, and a good many of us may wither before its blast. But it's God's own wind none the less, and a cleaner, better, stronger land will lie in the sunshine when the storm has cleared."

A black town car pulled up to the curb. Ellery wrapped the old chef in a long bear hug, then held the rear passenger door for him.

He tapped on the front window and, when the driver pressed the button to open it, said, "Start her up, my friend, for it's time that you were on your way."

The car pulled out into the pre-dawn traffic, leaving the hunched figure of Ellery Queen behind. He shivered in the crisp morning air, and looked to the east—where the wind, he knew, was gathering its forces. But as he stood there alone on the empty sidewalk, he felt reassured that—though he couldn't see it from here, deep within Manhattan's canyon of skyscrapers—it was in the east that the sun would always rise.

PART III

THE GRIFFENS
by Josh Pachter

E.Q. GRIFFEN EARNS HIS NAME

originally published in *Ellery Queen's Mystery Magazine* (December 1968)

INTRODUCTION BY FREDERIC DANNAY:

This is the three hundred and twenty-fifth "first story" to be published by Ellery Queen's Mystery Magazine, *another "first" by a teenager (God bless 'em!), coming less than two years after Dennis Dubin's "Elroy Quinn's Last Case" (July 1967). It is always a particularly happy event to welcome young blood to the circulatory system of the mystery story. (Now, let's have no talk about varicose veins; the mystery genre shows no sign whatever of hardening of the arteries!)*

At the time Josh Pachter wrote "E.Q. Griffen Earns His Name," he was sixteen years old, a junior at General Douglas MacArthur High School in Levittown, New York. (He is now a senior at Half Hollow Hills High School in Dix Hills, Huntington, New York.) The young author wrote: "My reigning passion is reading detective stories. Come to think of it, 'reading' is not the right word—I just eat *them. In fact, you might say that I'm addicted to the Queen's English, a Carr-nivore who Wolfes down every mystery I can get my Stout little hands on."*

Josh Pachter's chosen field is journalism, and he'd like to attend Columbia University. When not "eating detective stories," he bowls (a high of 229 at the time of this writing), trap- or skeetshoots, golfs, or works on his collection of Kuwaitian (!) postage stamps.

It should come as no surprise that Josh plans to continue with the characters in his first story—Inspector Ross Griffen and his eleven children, all named after detective heroes (and one heroine)—and has "roughed out" plots for Gideon Fell Griffen (who solves a locked car *murder) and Augustus Van Dusen Griffen (who solves a case less than ten seconds after hearing the details). Personally, we can't wait!*

For the third time in as many minutes, Ellery Queen removed his horn-rimmed glasses (they just don't *make* good pince-nez anymore) and carefully polished the lenses.

"Shades of Circe!" he muttered. "How can I be so abysmally dense?"

Ellery's vexation stemmed from his total inability to find the solution to a mystery that even John Hamish Watson would have been able to see through without the benefit of a second glance. But: "It's there," E.Q. groaned, "if only I knew what it was!"

"My goodness, Ellery," a feminine voice intruded, "don't tell me our little problem has got you talking to yourself?"

With a moan of embarrassment and despair, the great detective fled the room.

That Alison Field, he thought, as he paced the sidewalk in front of the Fields' home. *Why can't she realize that being a detective isn't as easy as it seems in books. It's hard work! I just* wish *I could show her!*

Ellery Queen's last name was Griffen, and he was sixteen years old.

About an hour before his hasty departure from the Fields' kitchen, Ellery had received a frantic telephone call from Mrs. Leora Field. "Ellery," she had said, "is anybody else home? Well, then, could *you* come over, please? Right away!"

When Ellery had arrived, the woman had led him into her kitchen and pointed a trembling finger at an open window. "They're gone! Do something, Ellery, they're gone!"

"What's gone?" the boy asked sensibly.

"My pies!" she shrieked. "My beautiful pies!"

Finally, the story came out. Leora Field had spent that day baking three large apple pies for a church bazaar to be held the next afternoon. Later, she had taken Alison, her only child, to a dental appointment, leaving the pies on the windowsill to cool. When they returned, the pies were missing.

Ellery's investigation had uncovered only one clue: an Italian postage stamp, which he found lying face down beneath the window. The stamp was golden brown and dark brown, and had been issued in 1964—Ellery had looked it up in his *Scott Catalogue.* The design of the stamp illustrated Italian sports.

Ellery reflected, and decided there were only four people known to him who could possibly be connected with foreign postage stamps: Charles Green, who owned the local stamp shop; Greg Zorn, a boy of Ellery's age who worked at Green's store every day after school; and two stamp collectors, Al Williams and Steve Holden. Steve's mother was in charge of the church bazaar.

Even though the Italian stamp seemed to be the only clue, Ellery simply could not figure out how to eliminate any of his suspects. A few phone calls established that not one of the four had an alibi for the crime period. And now Alison Field was needling him.

Suddenly a cry split the quiet late-afternoon air: "Ellery! *Ellery!*"

It was the detective's mother and, relieved, he trotted off toward home and dinner.

Something will hit me sooner or later, he thought.

The greatest compliment a Griffen child could receive was to be told that he had "earned his name."

Inspector Ross Griffen, of the Tyson County Police Force, had grown up on a rich diet of detective fiction and, in respectful memory of Sherlock Holmes, Hercule Poirot, Arsène Lupin, Bulldog Drummond and the other heroes of his youth, he had named each of his eleven children after one of them. And the inspector had introduced his sons and daughter to the joys of detection at early ages, teaching them to use their minds and wits to their fullest advantage.

A Griffen "earned his name" when he was able to solve a criminal problem in the manner of his namesake. Although these problems were usually made up round robin at the dinner table or read out of a book, the children had on several occasions used their detective powers to help solve cases their father had brought home with him.

Jane Marple Griffen, Peter Wimsey Griffen, Albert Campion Griffen, and John Jericho Griffen had pointed out clues that had led to the solution of two burglaries and one case of arson.

Parker Pyne Griffen, Gideon Fell Griffen, and Augustus Van Dusen Griffen had earned their names on make-believe crimes, while Sherlock Holmes, Perry Mason, and Nero Wolfe, being younger than ten years of age, had understandably not yet shown much creativity.

Inspector Griffen's biggest disappointment was Ellery. Not that the boy didn't try; he was always advancing ingenious theories, but he always seemed to be wrong.

So when, that Thursday evening, his father sat down at the table with a singularly puzzled and abstracted look on his face, Ellery kept quiet about his own problem and asked, "What's up, Dad?"

"Not now, El," the inspector answered. "I'll tell you about it after dinner."

But after dinner Griffen went into his study (a rare treat for a policeman with eleven children), and sat down with the phone. Hoping to get some information about their father's case, the Griffen children turned on the radio to an all-news station and listened. After the usual roundup of national and international news, the announcer delivered a local report:

"At an unknown time last night, Collier's Jewelers on South Firthson Avenue, under twenty-four-hour high-security guard, was broken into and robbed of a twenty-two-thousand-dollar diamond necklace. Police investigation, led by Inspector Ross Griffen, has thus far failed to discover the identity of the thief or thieves or how they managed to enter the building. The necklace was found missing this morning from a seemingly untouched display case by Geoffrey Collier, the store's owner and manager, during a routine search of the building. The police were immediately notified. Timothy Tierney, night guard, neither saw nor heard anything out of the ordinary last night. An intricate burglar-alarm system failed to go off. For further information on last night's robbery of Collier's Jewelers, stay tuned to...."

At the mention of the name Collier, Parker had sat up very straight and listened intently to the broadcast. At its conclusion, he exclaimed, "Boy! Anyone clever enough to get into Collier's is really going to be tough to catch."

"What do you mean, Park?" Jane asked.

"You know my friend Dickie Albert? Well, his brother Paul works at that jewelry store, and Paul was telling Dick and me about it. That place is as safe as Fort Knox."

"If this is Dad's case," Ellery put in, "we'd better know the layout. How about describing it to us?"

"From what Paul Albert told me, old man Collier has that whole place set up with just one purpose in mind: not letting any merchandise out of the store until it's been paid for. And up to now he's done a good job of it, too. So far, there have been three burglary attempts, and each time the crooks were caught before they even got into the store.

"Here's the way it works. Every night, before closing up, Collier locks all the windows from the inside. There are bars over each window on the outside. He double-locks the back door, and then, with Tierney standing guard outside, Collier searches the entire building. After the search, he double-locks the front door, gives the only duplicates of those two keys to Tierney, and leaves for home.

"When he comes back the next morning, Tierney unlocks the front door, returns the keys, and then the two of them search the store together. There's a series of alarms covering both doors, all the windows, and all the showcases. Like I said, safe as Fort Knox."

"Obviously not," Albert commented drily.

Augustus looked up from a magazine, yawned, and said, "It shouldn't require a Thinking Machine to inform you that, with all these precautions, it had to be an inside job."

Shaking his head, Parker replied, "I doubt it. According to Paul, Collier even put his porter through a strict security check. Believe me, anyone who can get a job at Collier's is one hundred percent honest. That guy Collier doesn't take any chances."

The study door opened, and Inspector Griffen walked out. He crossed the living room to his easy chair and dropped into it. Eyes closed, he slowly massaged his forehead. Finally he spoke: "All right, kids. If you're still interested, I'll tell you about the case."

"We kn-know most of the facts, D-d-dad," John Jericho stammered. Unlike his tall red-haired namesake, John was short, dark, and occasionally spoke with a stutter. "How about if we just ask q-q-questions about the points we're not clear on?"

"Fine with me, son," the inspector replied. "What would you like to know?"

"F-first of all, was the n-normal routine followed last night?"

"Yes, it was, everything as usual: windows and doors locked, et cetera."

"And the necklace was definitely in the case when Collier left?" Jane asked.

The inspector nodded, then elaborated. "It's by far the most valuable piece in the store, and Collier checks it just before he leaves. He's sure it was there last night."

Gideon, lost in thought until this time, looked up and said, "I rather think you've been ignoring the obvious. What about this man Tierney? People have gone rotten for far less than twenty-two thousand dollars. Money's the motive, the keys are the means, and Tierney had opportunity all last night."

"Collier stands by Tierney and every one of his other employees, but we're having them all checked out, anyway. I've got Captain Harris, my best man, on it, and I should be hearing from him any minute."

"I could explain this 'miracle' two other ways," continued Gideon, neither a doctor nor fat, but hoping to become the former and trying to stall off the latter. "Tierney could be innocent, but he could have left his post for a while—to get a beer, say—or even have dozed off for just long enough."

"I'll have all that information soon," the inspector said.

Albert spoke up: "Of course the burglar alarms were on all last night? No signs of tampering, nothing out of order?"

"Nothing," his father said. "There's a bell-and-light hookup at headquarters. If the alarm is tripped, or tampered with, the bell goes off, and, if there's any internal malfunction, the light starts flashing."

"What about those window bars?" Augustus asked.

"If I understand the point of your question, son, then the answer is no. Not even a circus midget could have passed between those bars. In fact, I think it would be safe to say that whoever got into Collier's Jewelers had a harder time of it than Professor Van Dusen had getting out of Cell 13."

A silence followed, shattered after some seconds by the ringing of the phone. Nero Wolfe Griffen rose, according to custom, and crossed to the kitchen. He picked up the receiver and, thanks to its long cord, was able to carry it back to his father.

"Hello, Griffen speaking ... yeah, Harris ... all of them? ... all night, huh? ... okay, thanks a lot." Inspector Griffen handed the phone back to his son, who walked once more to the kitchen.

Wolfe cradled the phone.

"Well, kids, that seems to let out Tierney," the inspector said. "Harris is convinced the night guard is completely innocent, and that he didn't leave his post all last night."

Inspector Griffen's eyes swept the room tiredly, then came to rest on Ellery. "What about you, El?" he asked. "You haven't said a word so far. Have you got any questions?"

"Just one, Dad," Ellery responded. "Whose fingerprints were found on the rifled display case?"

The inspector looked startled and replied, "It's funny you should ask that. We dusted every inch of that case, and it looks, according to what we found, like it just wasn't touched. Every print on it belonged there; there were no strange ones. Not a single area had been wiped off. And gloves seem to be out. Although wearing gloves will eliminate fingerprints, the gloves themselves leave marks or smudges on most materials. Not traceable to any particular pair, of course, but identifiable as having been made by gloves. That help you any, Ellery?"

"It might."

Inspector Griffen stood up. "Kids," he said, "I'm due back at headquarters at eight, and it's seven-thirty. Unless there are any suggestions, I'll leave now."

There were suggestions.

Jane said, "This reminds me of an incident that occurred back in high school, when Violet Bronson, a beautiful girl with deep blue—"

And Parker said, "The crime was quite obviously committed by some poor misguided—"

And Gideon said, "With all the doors and windows locked—"
And Augustus S.F.X. Van Dusen said, "Logically—"
And then, wonder of wonders, Ellery said, "I know the answer."

Inspector Griffen sat down heavily, breathed deeply, and listened to the silence. Finally he managed to ask, "What?"

"I said," Ellery repeated, "I know the answer. And I do. Not only do I know who robbed Collier's, but I know how and why."

"You're sure?" the inspector asked incredulously.

Ellery pulled off his glasses and thought for a moment. Then he nodded and said, "Yes, I'm sure."

"Then tell us, son."

"Of course. There are," he began, "two ways this crime could have been committed without leaving a single fingerprint, mark, or clue. The first is that the lack of clues indicates the lack of a crime—that is, the necklace was not stolen at all but merely mislaid."

"But we—" his father interrupted.

"Don't interrupt," Wolfe grumbled.

Ellery continued: "But we can eliminate this possibility, because a thorough police search failed to turn up the gems. Besides, they were definitely seen by Mr. Collier when he made his rounds last night.

"You especially, Sherlock, should know that 'when you have eliminated the impossible, whatever remains, however improbable, must be the truth.' So eliminating our first possibility indicates that the second one must be the truth. But before we discuss that, let's consider the ways in which the thief could have entered the store to commit the robbery.

"The front of Collier's," Ellery went on, "is guarded by Timothy Tierney, who has been found to be one hundred percent trustworthy. He remained at his post all night, making entry through the front impossible. There are other stores on both sides of the jewelry store, but with no connecting doors or partitions. The back windows were locked and barred, and found to have been undisturbed. The same goes for the back door, so rear entry can also be ruled out. I've been in the store, and I know that there are no other ways in—no fire escape, no skylight, no chimney. And we can't forget the burglar alarms—ready to go off at any intrusion.

"These facts all boil down to this: *There is no way that anyone could have entered Collier's after closing and stolen that necklace!*

"But since we have established that it *was* stolen, then the theft must have occurred *before* closing.

"Could the thief have taken the necklace and left before the building was locked up? No, since Collier saw it before closing up for the night.

"Could he have hidden in the building until after closing, stolen the jewels, and then left? Or waited until morning, managing to escape during the confusion caused by the discovery of the theft? No again: he would have been found during Collier's nightly search. And don't forget, no strange fingerprints were found on the display case."

"I've got it!" Jane cried. "Vickie Harding did the same thing up at the University. You know Vickie, Ellery, she's that cute girl with the long blond—"

"Get to the point, Jane!" snapped Peter, the oldest.

The Griffens' only girl blushed. "Oh, yes, sorry. I do ramble so. Anyway, one day last semester, Vickie forgot to bring her lunch to school. Rather than ask me for a loan so she could buy something in the cafeteria, she sneaked one of my sandwiches out of my lunch bag, leaving some crumpled-up paper in its place so that I wouldn't notice anything missing until later. Of course, I easily deduced that Vickie had taken the sandwich and confronted her. She broke down and confessed. I forgave her, and we've been the best of friends ever since."

"And just how does that help?" Parker sneered.

Jane looked at her younger brother furiously and continued, "Obviously the same thing happened here. The thief took the necklace before the store closed, leaving a paste replica in its place. Then, when Collier made his search, he thought the genuine necklace was still there!"

Parker clapped his hands with glee and pounced. "And just

what happened to this replica," he demanded. "Did it get up and walk away? Or did the successful diamond thief decide to come back later and steal the fake, too?"

Jane's mouth fell open.

"May I continue?" Ellery asked politely. "This brings us back to the second possibility—that the theft was committed before, not after, Collier's Jewelers was closed for the night.

"The biggest question still is: How was the necklace stolen without leaving either fingerprints or marks or smudges on the display case?

"But isn't it possible that we've been looking at this point from the wrong angle, that the thief's prints *are* on the case, and that we just didn't recognize them as belonging to the crook? In other words, that this *was* an inside job, after all?

"Assuming this to be true, the theft must have been committed *after* Mr. Collier looked into the case, but *before* the thief left the building."

Breaking his silence, Inspector Griffen said, "But, Ellery, Collier always conducts his search after all store personnel have already left."

"Exactly!" Ellery exclaimed triumphantly. "So it should be as clear as daylight that the thief must have been—"

"C-C-Collier!" John Jericho yelled.

"It's not too uncommon an occurrence," Inspector Griffen explained at breakfast the next morning. The jewelry-store owner had confessed, and the stolen necklace was now residing in a police safe.

"Collier had been backing a risky stock too heavily, and his firm was bankrupt. The brokers were pressing him to pay the large balance of his account, and he needed cash in a hurry. So Collier stole his own jewels, expecting to collect their full value from his insurance company, plus another five to ten thousand dollars by selling the diamonds through a fence."

"How did he manage it, Dad?" Albert asked.

"I told you that Collier and Tierney search the store together every morning, but Collier conducts the evening search by himself, with Tierney on guard outside. So it was easy for him to unlock the display case, slip the necklace into his pocket, and then relock the case. He probably figured that, even though Tierney had passed a rigorous security check, the guard would be blamed, since he had the perfect opportunity to commit the crime. But I suppose you deduced all this, Ellery. What I'd like to know is what put you on to it so quickly?"

Ellery beamed. "You know that Ellery Queen, after whom I'm named, often solves his cases through interpretation of seemingly insignificant clues: a piece of sugar in a dead man's hand, a cut-out piece of paper from the Sunday comics, a cryptic dying message.

"Well, Ellery once solved a case because there was no top hat where there should have been one, and another case when he noticed the statuette of a bridegroom missing from a newlywed's apartment. These two cases came to my mind when I realized that *this* case was also characterized by a lack of clues, by a clue that was missing.

"Finally, I realized that this *lack* of clues was a clue in itself, indicating that the theft must have been perpetrated by someone whose fingerprints on the display case would not be suspicious. This obviously pointed to an insider, and to the logical conclusion that it was Collier himself who stole the necklace."

"Ellery," Inspector Griffen said proudly, "you've earned your name."

Noon that day found Ellery Queen Griffen pounding on the front door of Leora Field's home. After a short while, Mrs. Field opened the door and ushered Ellery into the kitchen, where Mrs. Sandy Holden was sipping from a mug of steaming coffee.

"Ellery," she began, and coughed apologetically, "I think that little matter—"

The detective interrupted, "Yes, yes, that's why I'm here! I've got the case all solved! The answer hit me last night, after I managed to—ahem—clear up another slight matter. You see, that postage stamp was a blind! It was planted at the scene of the crime to throw suspicion on three innocent boys, your son included, Mrs. Holden."

"But, Ellery," Leora Field said.

"Just a minute, please. After deducing that this was all a frame-up, I began to wonder who could have possibly had access to that stamp—"

"But, Ellery," she said again.

"In a moment. I went through all the people I know, matching up motive and opportunity, but I got nowhere."

"Ellery!" Mrs. Field pleaded.

Paying no attention, the young criminologist continued: "Then I found someone. Someone who works every day in Benton's Grocery, which is *right next door to Green's Stamp Shop!* Peter Gould, who merely had to walk next door to purchase that stamp."

The victimized housewife looked at her friend, shrugged, and let Ellery go on.

"So it was Peter Gould who stole your pies, Peter Gould who planted that stamp, Peter Gould who—just the other day—told me that your daughter had refused to go to the movies with him! So, out of revenge, he tried to ruin your contribution to the church bazaar. The case," E.Q. concluded, "is solved!"

"Ellery," Mrs. Field said patiently, "there never was a case. This whole thing was just a big mistake."

"Excuse me?" Ellery said calmly.

"There never *was* a case, Ellery. Sandy—Mrs. Holden—came by to pick up those pies yesterday afternoon, but, as I told you, I was out with Alison. She didn't know that, though, so she went around back, thinking that I was here in the kitchen and perhaps couldn't hear the front doorbell. She saw the pies on the windowsill, and, when she realized I wasn't home, she took them. Peter Gould had nothing to do with it."

"But—but—" Ellery stammered. "My reasoning! There was nothing wrong with it! I—wait a second! What about that stamp?"

"I think I can explain that," Sandy Holden said. "I didn't want to take the pies without letting Leora know, so I left a note. You know that my son Steve collects postage stamps. Well, I picked that one up for him at Green's store, along with some others that Steve ordered, and they were all in a glassine envelope in my purse. When I was looking for a pencil and paper to leave the note—well, somehow the stamp must have fallen out."

"But the note!" Ellery insisted. "What about the note?"

"Oh," she continued, "I forgot. I wrote the note and put it on the kitchen table, this one right here. The breeze through the open window must have blown it off. When I came over for coffee this morning, I learned that Leora thought the pies had been stolen, and I explained the whole thing. We found the note over there in the corner."

"But," Ellery said, "but—"

"Sorry, Ellery, but I'm afraid you were all wrong."

"But," Ellery said, "but—"

"Oh, Ellery," Alison giggled from the doorway.

E.Q. GRIFFEN'S SECOND CASE

originally published in *Ellery Queen's Mystery Magazine* (May 1970)

INTRODUCTION BY FREDERIC DANNAY:

Josh Pachter's first story, "E.Q. Griffen Earns His Name," appeared in the December 1968 issue of EQMM; it was EQMM's three hundred and twenty-fifth "first story." The author was only sixteen years old when he wrote about Inspector Ross Griffen of the Tyson County Police Force, a widower with eleven children, all of whom had been named after detective heroes (and one heroine) of his youthful reading (with one anachronism, which we leave it to you to spot). Thus, the Griffen children, helping to solve cases in which their father was involved, "earned" their famous first and middle names—Jane Marple, Peter Wimsey, Albert Campion, John Jericho, Parker Pyne, Gideon Fell, Augustus Van Dusen, Sherlock Holmes, Perry Mason, Nero Wolfe, and the hero of Josh Pachter's "first story," Ellery Queen Griffen.

Naturally, young Mr. Pachter plans to write more stories about all of the Griffen children; but before getting to Gideon, Augustus, Sherlock, Nero, et al., he has written a "second case" about Ellery. (And who are we to complain?)

When he finished and submitted "E.Q. Griffen's Second Case," Josh Pachter was seventeen years old (ah, happy time—and what a lesson to dropouts!), and to celebrate his eighteenth birthday, in September 1969, Josh "changed his scholastic status from high-school senior to freshman at the University of Michigan," where he is now "studying Honors Journalism."

But however hard young Mr. Pachter may be studying journalism, we are sure he will find time for more adventures of Inspector Ross Griffen's children, and especially of "Ellery in Queenland"....

As Garrett Conway strolled casually along the early-morning street, the large bronze medallion that hung around his neck jounced up and down, conspicuously dark against the bright yellows, pinks, and blues of his gaudy metallic Nehru jacket. He wore enormously flared bellbottomed trousers held up by a low-slung leather garrison belt, the huge buckle almost menacing against the psychedelic gaiety of the rest of his attire.

Conway's mod appearance did not end with his clothing. His hair was long and unkempt, and he wore a pair of scraggly pre-Civil War mutton chop sideburns. Even though he was clean, an impartial observer would have sworn he needed a bath.

Garrett Conway was, of course, a hippie. He was not a protesting sit-, stand-, or love-in radical, and he did not play the guitar or sitar. And, since he did not meditate, transubstantiate, or hallucinate, the man had only one way left to prove his hip nonconformity to the world.

Garrett Conway was a poet.

He wrote free verse without realizing it had ever been liberated; his poems had a certain meter and rhythm, even though his definitions of those terms would have left much to be desired in the way of academic accuracy.

Conway slaved over his poetry, and when a work was completed he submitted it to any one of a number of literary magazines, which immediately rejected it. His career was a succession of submissions and rejections *ad infinitum*.

In the field of serious poetry, Conway remained unpublished, but he did not live in a garret, and he did not starve. He had no objection to sacrificing his ideals to maintain his health, and he was one of the ten or twelve most successful authors of juveniles in the United States. When he needed money, the poet ground out a rhyming kiddie book that would be snapped up by whichever one of his publishers he chose to send it to.

Garrett Conway, unpublished serious poet, walked along the deserted street, and his medallion bounced against his chest, and he never heard the shadowy figure steal up behind him and stab him fiercely in the back.

Conway crumpled to the sidewalk, and the figure knelt over his inert body and rapidly searched his wallet and the contents of his pockets. At last the figure rose and, smiling at the effect of the dark red stain on his victim's Nehru jacket, disappeared into the night.

The poet lay still, then finally stirred. He dragged himself to the edge of the sidewalk and, his mind long familiar with the doings of children, painfully detached a loose strip of tar separating two sections of the concrete curb.

Using the tar on the cement, Conway began to write. He made several strokes with his tar pencil, and then he coughed up a small amount of blood and died.

The message on the scrap of paper read, "Graphology is nonsense. You can't tell character from a person's handwriting!" The note was signed "Augustus S.F.X. Van Dusen Griffen."

Ellery Queen Griffen looked up from the piece of paper and said, "Of course I don't agree with what you've written, Augie, but the *way* you wrote it is very revealing."

"Come on, El," his older brother scoffed, "you can't be serious!"

Five of Inspector Ross Griffen's eleven children were scattered around their father's spacious living room. Jane Marple and Peter Wimsey would not return home from college until the next month's intersession. Parker Pyne was in the process of shutting out a rival high-school baseball team, and Albert Campion, Perry Mason, and Nero Wolfe had just left to spend the weekend with their Uncle James, Ross Griffen's younger brother and an aspiring author.

"I am *so* serious," Ellery replied heatedly. "Just give me a chance, and I'll analyze your handwriting right now."

Augustus, resigned, conceded. "All right, go ahead."

"Now, then," E.Q. began, "there are thirteen main factors to be considered when you analyze a person's handwriting: size, slope, style, thickness, and so on. Each factor means little by itself, but when combined with the other twelve you can get a pretty accurate character chart. Your writing, Augie, is medium-sized, and all the—"

Inspector Griffen entered the room and shouted a hearty "Hi!" to his children.

"Hiya, Dad," they answered in unison.

Griffen asked, "What are you kids doing?"

"Ellery's teaching us graphology," Augustus chuckled. "He's read a couple of books, and now he thinks he's an expert."

"A couple of books!" exclaimed Ellery, his nostrils flaring. "I've studied Josef Ranald, Dorothy Sara, Klara G. Roman, Rudolph Hearns, Billy Pesin Rosen—"

"So what?" said Gideon Fell, supporting the Thinking Machine's skepticism.

Ignoring the jibe, Ellery continued modestly, "And I myself have written a trifling English composition on the subject, in which I go into a detailed discussion of some seventy-two handwriting traits."

"But look, Ellery," Augustus commented, "you've known me all your life. You could 'deduce' lots of facts about me through graphology, even if you never—"

"What?" Ellery sputtered. "Are you accusing me of—?"

Inspector Griffen quickly intervened. "Sorry to break this up, guys, but it's getting late. How'd you kids like to do something tonight? What about a movie?"

Gideon Fell looked up from the newspaper. "Gee, Kaye Chesterton's new picture is playing at the Majestic tonight. We could go see that."

John Jericho laughed. "K-Kaye Chesterton! Don't you ever think about anything but that t-t-two-bit so-called actress?"

The telephone rang.

Inspector Griffen walked into the kitchen and lifted the receiver. He listened intently for several minutes, his off-duty smile dissolving into a scowl. He slammed down the phone.

"Sorry, kids, I've got to get back to headquarters. We'll have to save the movie for tomorrow."

"What's wrong, Dad?" asked Sherlock Holmes, the youngest of the children.

"There was a homicide early this morning," his father explained, "and I thought we had it all wrapped up. Now it looks like we're going to have some problems, after all."

"Can't you tell us about it before you go?" asked Gideon Fell eagerly.

The inspector looked at his watch, shrugged, and dropped into a chair.

"Sometimes I think you kids are worth more than the whole Tyson County police force," he said. "Just after one this morning, we got an almost incoherent call from a Leonard Goldberg reporting a corpse on Truxton Boulevard. Goldberg had been walking home from a poker game when he discovered the body. A two-man team was immediately dispatched...."

A man was waving wildly from the sidewalk, and the patrol car swerved, coming to a stop by the man's side.

"Goldberg?" Sergeant Verini asked.

"Yes, sir," the man responded, "Lenny Goldberg. Look at—he's dead, officer!"

"That's for us to say," Verini said. He bent over the crumpled mass of colors. "D.O.A.," he pronounced coldly.

" ... there was a small, thin piece of tar clutched in the dead man's hand. The victim had used it as a crude sort of pencil—"

"A dying message," Ellery said ecstatically. "What did it say?"

The inspector smiled grimly and removed a slip of paper from his jacket pocket. He unfolded it and held it up for his children's inspection....

"Hey, Bob," Verini called to his partner, "take a look at this."

Patrolman Robert Lanaro looked down at the concrete in front of the still unidentified corpse. Involuntarily, he let out a long, low whistle as he stared at the message scrawled quite legibly on the cement.

"As you can see," Griffen continued, "it's just the numbers one, two, and three, written shakily but distinctly, and of a uniform size."

"B-but what does it mean?" John Jericho asked.

"Oh, we know what it means. Once we identified the victim and checked into his background, the meaning of his dying message became obvious."

Inspector Griffen settled back in his chair and tented his fingers.

"Garrett Conway," he said. "That's the name of our young dead beatnik, or hippie, or whatever you kids call them these days. He was thirty-five, lived by himself in a four-room apartment on Ryder, pretty high-class for a hippie. Conway made a very good living writing children's books, but his big ambition was to write serious poetry. He's pretty good with the kiddie stuff—you used to like his books, Sherlock—but I've been told his adult work is third-rate."

"And the dying message?" murmured Ellery. "What does it mean?"

"Well, whenever a cop sees a series of numbers like that, the first thing he does is make a simple alphabet substitution. You've done it yourself, Ellery: A for one, B for two, and so on. If you translate one-two-three into letters, there are three possibilities: one-two-three gives ABC, twelve-three gives LC, and one-twenty-three gives AW.

"And when we checked out Conway's known associates, the first thing we found is that his closest friend is named Andrew Brandon Channing.

"So Conway, near death, translated his murderer's initials into numbers, leaving us a clue to the identity of his killer. Was it Channing? The message indicated him, so we put out an APB. He was picked up several hours ago, boarding a bus for Boston. He claimed he was going to visit his fiancée, Leila Sasloe, but we reached her by phone and she said she wasn't expecting him. Channing insisted he was planning to surprise her, but we felt justified in holding him for questioning.

"We can't get a thing out of him, though," Griffen concluded. "He says he left his apartment around ten last night, strolled around town for several hours, and then went home to bed. He can't prove it, but we can't prove otherwise."

"Tell us some more about Channing," Gideon said.

"Unfortunately," his father admitted, "there's not much to tell. Channing's record is entirely clean—not so much as a parking ticket. He graduated with honors from an Ivy League university, came here to work on the *News*, and is happily engaged to Miss Leila Sasloe, a girl he grew up with in Boston, his hometown.

"He was very close to Garrett Conway—in fact, Conway was to be his best man when he marries the Sasloe girl next month. Andrew Channing had absolutely no motive for killing Garrett Conway.

"But Conway as good as named him as his murderer. We've run that one-two-three through the wringer, and the only way it makes sense is the obvious one—as Channing's initials."

"But, Dad," said Ellery, "why did Conway have to disguise the initials? Why didn't he just write ABC, or even the name Channing? Why do it the hard way?"

"I don't know, son," Griffen answered. "A dying man's mind often works in strange ways, as you well know from reading the original Ellery Queen books. Perhaps Conway was afraid that Channing might return and, seeing his initials or name on the sidewalk, rub the letters out. Whatever the reason, the meaning of the message is clear. It just doesn't make sense any other way.

"Now, unless one of you kids can tell me how to *prove* that Andrew Channing is a murderer, I'll be off to headquarters."

"I've got it!" said Ellery excitedly. "Just let me examine a sample of Channing's handwriting, and I'll be able to tell you if he's capable of committing murder. If he isn't, you can investigate elsewhere, but, if he is, maybe confronting him with an analysis of his handwriting will make him confess!"

"Come on now, Ellery," the inspector said sternly, "this graphology of yours is all right for fun and games, but this is serious."

"But it works, Dad! It really does!"

"No," said the inspector.

"I did pretty well on that Collier robbery."

"Well," said the inspector.

"It can't hurt to let me try, can it?"

"Oh, come along."

*

Inspector and Ellery Griffen entered the still-busy Tyson County Justice Building and headed for the Criminal Division.

"Wait a minute, Dad," Ellery said. "Before we see Channing, could I get a look at the clothing Conway was wearing when he was stabbed?"

"Why?" the inspector asked.

"You called Garrett Conway a hippie," the boy explained. "I'd like to see what you meant."

"I don't see why not," the inspector shrugged, reversing direction and leading his son to a frosted-glass door they had previously passed. "In here," he said.

The Griffens entered the almost-barren room and stepped to a large table. Carefully laid out on the table were Garrett Conway's clothes, glorious even after their wearer's death.

As the inspector looked on with interest, Ellery examined the bloodstained Nehru jacket, the bellbottomed trousers, the bronze medallion, and the worn leather boots. He picked up the World War II garrison belt, then turned to his father and asked, "Didn't he have anything in his pockets?"

"Just the usual stuff: keys, change, handkerchief, you know."

Ellery gently put the leather belt back on the table and glanced again at Conway's clothes. "At least he looked like a hippie."

The interrogation room of the Tyson County Criminal Division was occupied by three men. One, dressed almost casually in a brown herringbone sport coat and tan slacks, his tie loose and collar undone, stood at the end of a long table and was firing questions at the second man, who was seated, sweating, and scared. The third man, tie and suit jacket draped over his knee, was slumped in a wooden chair in a corner of the room, punctuating his partner's questioning with an occasional snore.

Inspector Griffen slammed the door, and the sleeping man awoke with a start, surveyed the scene, then arose and crossed to the inspector's side.

"Hi, Greg," Ellery's father addressed him. "Anything?"

"Not any," the man admitted, struggling into his jacket. Indicating the seated prisoner, he added, "Channing here won't give us a thing, sir."

"I've got nothing to give," Andrew Channing flamed. "I did *not* kill Garrett Conway. He was my best friend. I haven't *seen* him since the day before yesterday. I've already *told* you, again and again!"

"Channing," the questioner continued, "if you didn't murder Conway, then what did those numbers he wrote mean? He practically named you as—"

"I don't know *what* they mean," Channing interrupted. "I just know I didn't kill Garrett."

Ellery whispered, "Dad," and the inspector bent down. Then he straightened and said, "Sorry, son, it slipped my mind."

Nodding to the two detectives in turn, Griffen said, "This is Lieutenant Greg Sunn, and Sergeant Thomas Verini. Sergeant Verini was the first of my men to see Conway. Greg, Tom, my boy Ellery. He thinks he's going to wrap this case up for us."

"Inspector," Verini protested, "this isn't a—"

"Tom, if it hadn't been for Ellery, Geoffrey Collier would probably be a free and considerably wealthier man today. The boy has an idea, and I've decided to let him try it. What have we got to lose?"

"But—" Verini began.

"Any objections?" Griffen said coldly.

The sergeant muttered, "No, sir."

Greg Sunn, older and wiser than his by-the-book partner, smiled and said, "Well, Ellery, it's about time *somebody* closed the book on this case."

"And exactly how do you plan to solve it for us?" asked Verini, much too politely.

"He's a graphologist," Inspector Griffen explained. "He's going to look at a sample of Channing's penmanship and tell us whether or not he murdered Conway. Would you object to that type of examination, Mr. Channing?"

The suspect looked up, shook his head, and said, "Anything that'll get me out of this place!"

"Then go to it, lad," Lieutenant Sunn said cheerfully.

The boy smiled and pulled a bedraggled pad of paper from his hip pocket. He placed the pad before Channing and handed the suspect a ballpoint pen.

"What do I do?" the man asked warily.

"Just write," Ellery instructed. "Anything that comes into your head, and then sign it."

Channing put one end of the pen to his chin and stared at the blank sheet. Finally, he began to write—slowly, laboriously, carefully holding the pad in place with his free hand. He finished, and silently returned the pad and pen to the young detective.

Ellery ripped the top sheet from the pad and studied it, making notes on the next page. After several minutes of scrutiny, he said, "I think this should just about do it."

Verini and Sunn stared incredulously at the boy.

Passing the suspect's note to his father, Ellery continued: "Look at Channing's handwriting, Dad. There are many important characteristics that contribute to my conclusion, but I'll just point out a few of them to give you the overall picture.

"Channing's weak descending finals, combined with his small signature—which slants the wrong way for a righty—tell me that he feels unjustly oppressed, and that this oppression probably involves money. Add to that the extensive use of heavy strokes and large capitals, and I see that he longs to rid himself of his oppressor ... and that he won't let consideration for others stand in his way."

Inspector Griffen signaled to his subordinates, and they joined him. The three of them conferred briefly, and the puzzled look on the inspector's face was soon matched by two others. Ellery's father seemed about to speak, then shook his head.

"I'll just mention two more items," the boy went on. "The way his looped letters slant to the left, and the period he put after his signature. Those are sure signs of a vicious nature."

Sergeant Verini stabbed a finger at the sheet of paper and whispered heatedly to the inspector. Griffen nodded, but remained silent.

"Graphology never lies," said E.Q., "and, after examining Andrew B. Channing's handwriting, I believe I can explain what must have happened early this morning—the events leading up to Garrett Conway's murder."

"Inspector!" Verini protested angrily.

"Quiet," Griffen commanded.

Ellery continued confidently: "You were being unjustly oppressed, Mr. Channing, and the oppression involved money. The oppressor was your 'best friend,' Garrett Conway. I suppose Conway was blackmailing you, and you wanted out. But what grounds did Conway have for blackmail? You've got a completely clean record—what had you done wrong?

"You hadn't done *anything* wrong, had you, Mr. Channing? But you *would* have—if you married Leila Sasloe.

"Your marrying Miss Sasloe would have been a crime, wouldn't it? But you thought no one would ever know, and you were willing to take the risk."

"Ellery," Inspector Griffen asked, "what crime are you talking about?"

"Bigamy," the boy replied. "If I'm right, and I'm sure I am, Channing is already married. When he was going to that Ivy League university you mentioned, Channing was indiscreet with a girl he—let me finish, Dad. He finally had to marry her, but they managed to keep the whole thing a big secret. His wife probably miscarried—please, Dad, I'm not a—"

"Inspector Griffen," Lieutenant Sunn said quickly, "I think I have to agree with Sergeant Verini. This is getting a little out of—"

"Go on, Ellery," said the inspector.

"Thanks, Dad. As I was about to say, after Channing's wife miscarried, he deserted her. Later, when Channing decided to marry the girl next door, he didn't think anyone knew about his running out on—"

"How *did* Conway know?" Verini demanded.

"I have no idea, and it's not important. He *did* know, and he had proof and was blackmailing Channing.

"So Channing waited for his opportunity, and this morning it came. Perhaps, Mr. Channing, you were waiting outside Conway's apartment house. It doesn't really matter—you followed him, and finally the coast was clear. You crept up behind Conway, the man who had the power to ruin your life. You raised your arm—and stabbed him. And, as you watched Conway slump to the ground, blood flowing from his wound, you stooped over him."

Inspector Griffen flinched, and Verini's scowl deepened, but the three officers remained silent. Andrew Channing did not move, but there was an amused half-smile on his face.

Ellery continued: "You pulled the murder weapon from his body, wiped it clean, and put it in your pocket, to be disposed of later. Then you searched the body—but you didn't find what you were looking for.

"Before you left the scene, did you stand there admiring your work, Mr. Channing? How long did you stand over the body, staring down at what you had done?"

The accused man's smile slowly faded. Inspector Griffen and Lieutenant Sunn looked at each other, as Sergeant Verini stood Velie-speechless.

"How long?" Ellery demanded. "And did you just *stand* there, or did you touch the still-warm body? Did you feel the—?"

Calm fleeing, the suspect whispered, "No! Stop! Stop it! I didn't—I did *not* kill Garrett Conway! You're lying! I was never married before! You can't prove—Garrett was my best friend, I tell you!"

Ellery stepped to Andrew Channing's side and said, too softly for anyone else to hear, "Martha Horton."

And Andrew Brandon Channing collapsed, sobbing, on the interrogation-room floor.

Ellery Queen Griffen lay in bed, reflecting on the events of the day. He had demonstrated to his brother Augustus the value of graphology, and he had caused Andrew Channing to confess both to a secret marriage to Martha Horton, whom he had later deserted, and to the premeditated murder of Garrett Conway.

And Ellery thought, *Maybe Augie won't be so quick to criticize me now. Maybe he'll realize that being older doesn't automatically make him right.*

But I guess I'd better lay off the graphology bit, though. If I'd really analyzed Channing's writing instead of faking it, I'd've had to say that he was innocent. His handwriting indicates a timid, affectionate man who is cautious, prudent, and avoids physical conflict at all cost.

But since Garrett Conway's dying message told me where to find conclusive proof of Channing's guilt, I decided to use graphology to make the killer confess—just to teach Augustus a lesson!

The answer, Ellery wrote, *obviously lay in Conway's dying message. As a long-time fan of my namesake's writing, I've learned not to take any such message at face value. My father couldn't think of any possible meaning for that "one-two-three" except the coincidental one of Andrew Brandon Channing's initials, but he never considered the possibility that "one-two-three" might not have been the entire message.*

Ellery turned a page of his diary and continued to write:

In the original Ellery Queen's "GI Story," a dying father left the message "GI," which seemed to indicate that his killer was a soldier, implicating one of his three sons. That's what gave me the idea. Like the victim in "GI Story," Garrett Conway died before he could finish writing his message. But I can't blame Dad for missing that big point. He hasn't read Ellery Queen for quite a while. And besides, Conway was a children's poet, and he was trying to write a children's poem—and, no matter how smart Dad is, he's not a child.

The message seemed an obvious reference to Andrew Brandon Channing, but its third symbol was not *meant to be the numeral three. If Conway had lived a little longer, he would have had time to put his tar pencil at the top-left end of that "three" and draw a straight line down to the bottom-left end—turning the number into the letter B.*

I thought that writing Channing's initials as numbers was a little too pat, and so did Dad. But where he tried to find another meaning for "one-two-three" and failed, it took an Ellery Queen to see that the message was intended to be "one-two-B" … and a child to realize that kiddie-poet Conway, until death stopped him, was trying to write the first line of one of Mother Goose's counting rhymes.

"One, two," Ellery said aloud as he wrote, "buckle my shoe."

*

"Conway's shoes didn't have buckles," Ellery said, handing a piece of paper to his father. "But his garrison belt had a big one, and cleverly hidden in the back of the belt buckle was a wad of folded paper—this photocopy of a marriage license for Andrew Channing and Martha Horton.

"So the dying man's last message wasn't merely a clue to his killer's name. It was a treasure map, telling you where to find evidence—concrete proof of the murderer's motive."

"And why didn't you just show me your proof in the first place?" Inspector Griffen asked, his voice stern.

"I guess I should have," Ellery admitted. "But I wanted to prove to Augie that graphology is a valuable science, not just a pastime. Unfortunately, Channing's handwriting was completely devoid of criminal indications, so I had to fake my analysis. And even *that* wasn't enough, so I had to let him know that I had found the copy of his marriage license in order to get him to confess."

"But Ellery," Griffen said, "there's still one thing I don't understand. Last night, you asked me why Conway wrote Channing's initials in a kind of cipher—well, disguised, anyway—instead of simply writing ABC. Well, why did the dying man go through the rigmarole of writing the beginning of a nursery rhyme? Why didn't he simply write—or start to write—the word 'buckle'?"

"For the same reason you gave last night, Dad. You suggested that the murderer might return to the scene and, seeing his initials on the concrete, rub them out. If Conway wrote 'buckle' and Channing came back and spotted it, he would have known just where to look, and he would have found the hiding place and the photocopy. But a nursery rhyme would probably strike him as the meaningless scrawl of a dying children's poet."

Inspector Griffen turned solemn. "Well, son," he said, "you withheld important evidence in a murder case, but you *did* get Channing to confess. I'll let you off this time, but I don't *ever* want to catch you pulling a stunt like this again!"

And, for the first time in a very long while, Ellery Queen submitted meekly to the wishes of his father, the inspector.

SAM BURIED CAESAR

originally published in *Ellery Queen's Mystery Magazine* (August 1971)

INTRODUCTION BY FREDERIC DANNAY:

Josh Pachter, you will recall, is the creator of Inspector Ross Griffen of the Tyson County Police Force, a widower with eleven children, all of whom he has named after detective heroes (and one heroine) of his youthful reading. The first and middle names of the ten sons are Peter Wimsey, Albert Campion, John Jericho, Parker Pyne, Gideon Fell, Augustus Van Dusen, Sherlock Holmes, Perry Mason, Ellery Queen, and Nero Wolfe. The only daughter is named Jane Marple Griffen.

You will also recall that Mr. Pachter has already given us two cases about E.Q. Griffen (December 1968 and May 1970). Now he gives us the first recorded case about ten-year-old Nero Wolfe Griffen and his best friend, Archie Goodwin—oops, pardon, Artie Goodman—an undeniably Neroish and Wolfean investigation....

Josh Pachter was eighteen years old when he wrote "Sam Buried Caesar." What will he write when he is twenty-eight? When he is thirty-eight? The mind boggles....

For the fifty-millionth time, my name is *not* Archie Goodwin! It's *Artie,* Artie *Goodman*—Arthur Eliot Goodman, Junior, to be exact. But ever since we moved in next door to Inspector Ross Griffen and his brood about a year ago, and ten-year-old Nero Wolfe and I became best friends, I've been Archie Goodwin to everyone in town.

Not that I mind the comparison, you understand. Nero got me interested in the Wolfe stories, and I've read most of them by now; Archie's pretty cool and everything, even though he keeps talking about these dumb *girls* all the time, but it's just that I don't want to be typed as Nero Griffen's legman for the rest of my life.

I mean, I'm pretty smart myself, you know. I was the one who found Lou Kramer's missing bicycle, not Nero, and if it wasn't for me asking the right question at the right time, we never would have discovered who was shoplifting from Mr. Tierney's five-and-dime.

And even though Wolfe beat me to it, without so much as getting out of his chair, I did solve the mystery of Sam Cabot's dog Caesar all on my own.

It was the end of June, about a week after Wolfe had gotten out of fourth grade and I'd escaped from third, when we decided to form our own detective agency. I kind of liked "Griffen and Goodman, Private Investigators," myself, but Nero insisted on "The Nero Wolfe Detective Service" and I didn't make a fuss—I'd gone along with the idea for the fun of it, anyway, not for the glory.

Our first couple of days were pretty slow, but soon the word got around and cases started leaking in—mostly lost toys and things, nothing really interesting at first. Nero proved pretty good at tracking down that kind of stuff, and we began to build up a reputation of sorts. After three weeks, we risked raising our retainer from a dime to fifteen cents, and nobody seemed to mind.

Somewhere along the line, Nero's brother Sherlock got into the act. He wasn't much good, but he didn't bother anyone, so we let him hang around until the day he deduced, from a rip in my shirt and the dirt under my fingernails, that *I* was the one who'd been swiping apples from the tree in Jerry Tieger's back yard. At that point, we decided that Sherlock had to go—actually, *I* decided that either he went or I did, and Wolfe agreed that my detective abilities were more important than mere family ties.

So Sherlock was banished from the agency, and Nero and I went back to handling our couple of cases a day, all by ourselves. We averaged thirty-five to forty cents a case, and more from grown-ups, plus expenses—which was nowhere near as profitable as a good paper route but lots more enjoyable.

Agency business took up most of our time, and as a result we didn't get to see old friends as often as we used to. I hadn't spoken to Sam Cabot in weeks when I walked into the Griffen garage, our office, one morning in August and found him seated in one of the yellow folding chairs we kept around for clients.

"Hi, Archie," Sam said, with a mournful look on his face.

"Artie," I said automatically. "Hi, Sam. What's up?"

"I just finished telling Nero," Sam answered. "It's about my dog."

"Caesar?"

"Sure, Caesar!" Sam exploded. "He's my dog, isn't he? I—I mean, he *was* my dog."

I pounced. "What do you mean, *was* your dog? Has something happened to him?"

"You're sharp as a tack today, aren't you, Artie?" Nero chuckled. "Sam, you'd better go back to the beginning and fill my partner in."

"There's not much to tell," Sam began slowly. "I was out playing with Caesar about three hours ago, at that vacant field at the corner of Hoover and Berkshire. I was throwing a rubber ball around, and Caesar was fielding. Well, the ball got away from me and rolled into Berkshire, and Caesar ran after it. There's a thirty-mile-an-hour speed limit there, but this late-model, off-white convertible came tearing down Hoover, doing fifty at least, and made the turn into Berkshire without even slowing down. The driver must have seen Caesar, because he slammed on his brakes, but he was too late—he hit him. The guy started to pull over, then he changed his mind and beat it."

"Did you get his license-plate number?" I asked.

"He was going too fast. They were out-of-state plates, I could see that, and I think the last number was a three or an eight, but I'm not sure. Anyway, I was too worried about Caesar to think much about the car. I ran up to him. I remember looking around for help and not seeing any other people or cars nearby, so I dragged him to the sidewalk, off the street.

"There was blood all over the place. I felt for his heartbeat, but I couldn't find it. Caesar was dead."

Sam slowly shook his head from side to side. He didn't look like he was going to be doing any more talking for a while, so I shifted my glance to Nero.

"Sam then moved the corpse to a corner of the vacant field," Nero told me, "and ran home to tell his parents what had happened and to find out what he should do. There was no one home."

"I—I couldn't just leave him there, lying around with blood all over him and everything," Sam sniffled, "so I took a shovel and went back to the vacant field and dug a big hole and buried him. After I filled in the hole, I just stood there for a while and, well, cried. I loved that dog, Archie!"

"Artie," I said. "So you want us to find out who killed your dog?"

"There's more to the story," Nero frowned. "Go on, Sam."

"Well, I f-finally went home and sort of mooned around for a while. Then I decided to go back and get Caesar's collars and tags, so I'd have something to remember him by. So I went to the field and dug up the grave and—and—"

"And what?" I prompted.

"And Caesar's body was gone."

"What!" I yelled.

"You heard him, Artie," Nero growled. "He dug up the grave, and the dog's body was gone."

"He must have dug in the wrong place," I said.

"No!" Sam cried. "I didn't!"

Nero leaned back.

"This is about where you came in, Artie," he said. "Sam was telling me that, because it hasn't rained around here in almost a week, the top layer of dirt at the vacant field has turned a kind of dry, dusty, light brown. When he dug the hole and buried Caesar, moister dark-brown dirt from underneath got left on top of the grave. Sam?"

"So when I went back for the collar and tags," our client said, "I just looked for the spot where the dirt was dark-brown instead of light, and dug there. And Caesar was gone."

"Do you have any idea why someone would want to steal Caesar's corpse?" I asked.

"No, I can't see why *anyone* would do a thing like that! I can't figure it out at all!" Sam's voice trembled.

"Who knew where you buried your dog?"

"No one—well, I didn't *tell* anyone, not even that he was dead. But I guess a few people walked by while I was digging the grave, and some cars must have passed by, too, and they might have seen what I was doing."

"Did you recognize any of the people or cars that passed?"

"No, none. But I wasn't looking at them carefully or anything."

"Could the convertible that killed Caesar have been one of the cars that passed?" Nero asked.

"I—I didn't notice, really. I don't think so."

"What about the driver?" I said. "Could he have been one of the people who walked by?"

"I guess so. I don't know. I just wasn't paying much attention to anything except Caesar."

"All right, Sam," Nero said, rising, "that's all we need to hear right now. We'll take your case."

"You'll find out who killed Caesar?" Sam asked eagerly.

"No promises. But we'll do our best."

"And you'll get the body back?"

"We'll try. Our retainer is fifteen cents, which you can give to Artie. Of course, the final fee will depend on our results. We'll get back to you as soon as we can, maybe today or tomorrow."

Sam got up from his yellow chair.

"Thanks, Nero," he said, shaking Wolfe's hand good-bye. "I really mean it, thanks a lot."

Then he handed me a sticky dime and a nickel, shook my hand, and said, "You, too, Archie. Thanks."

"Artie," I said, as I pocketed the coins and ushered Sam out of our office.

Numbers have always fascinated me.

Like, did you know that if you multiply any number, any number at all, by nine, and then add up the digits of the product, and then add up the digits of that sum, and keep adding until you wind up with a single digit, that final digit will *always* be nine?

Or did you ever notice that, out of all the millions of squiggles that *could* have been chosen to represent our ten numerals from zero to nine, two of the ten that *were* chosen happened to be shaped exactly the same? The only difference between a six and a nine is that one of them—and I wish I knew which one—is upside down.

That particular afternoon, as I pedaled along Berkshire toward Hoover and the vacant field, I was thinking about how a three is just an eight with the left side sliced off, and how it would be easy to mix up a three and an eight if your mind was on something else and you only got a quick look. People get confused when they're worried about the life of a loved one, I thought, even when the loved one is an animal, and they can't be expected to pay attention to trivial details. Still, I wished Sam could have been more definite about the license plate of that convertible.

After Sam Cabot left the Griffen garage, Nero and I had tried to figure out why anyone would want to steal the body of a dead dog. Even alive, Caesar was just a scrawny little dachshund, not worth much of anything. Why was he so important now that he was dead?

The most logical answer seemed to be that the hit-and-run driver felt that somehow he could be identified through the corpse of his victim, so he had returned to the scene of his crime and removed the incriminating corpse. It didn't make much sense, but that was the best we could come up with, so my job was now to investigate the scene for clues, and then to hunt for an off-white, late-model convertible with out-of-state plates and a license number ending in either a three or an eight.

I braked at the corner of Berkshire and Hoover and got off my bicycle, leaving it on the sidewalk with the kickstand down.

Carrying a shovel in my right hand, I explored the vacant field. Most of the lot was nothing more than the dusty light-brown dirt that Sam had described, with small patches of weeds and crabgrass here and there and yellowed papers and slivers of glass scattered all around. Two sides of the field were open, bordering on Berkshire and Hoover, and the other sides were separated from the adjoining lots by a tall wooden fence.

I quickly located the circular patch of dark, recently turned earth that showed where Sam had buried the dead body of his dog and began digging. After twenty minutes or so, I had hollowed out a hole about four feet deep and found nothing but four feet of dirt. Satisfied that Caesar was indeed not where he was supposed to be, I filled in the hole and went back to my bicycle.

This may sound a lot like second guessing now, but as I climbed on my bike I took a good look around, and I got the funniest feeling that something was missing, something *besides* the body I'd been looking for. You know how it is—you know something is wrong, but you just can't pin it down. Something was missing, something that *should* have been there, and I sat for a while trying to figure out what the heck it was. Finally I shrugged and, giving up for the time being, pushed off.

I rode around town for a long time, looking for the murder car. I saw off-white convertibles with in-state plates, and out-of-state plates on old off-white sedans, but I drew a blank on late-model, off-white converts with the right kind of plates. Even *without* the three or eight at the end of the number.

Disappointed, I turned back to the road. But while I'd been looking in different directions I'd been steering blind, and now I found myself heading straight for a parked station wagon. I swerved toward the curb and backpedaled hard, trying to avoid a crash. At the last second, I closed my eyes.

There was a sharp jolt as I smacked into something, and I spilled off my bicycle onto the sidewalk. I opened my eyes and saw that I had missed the station wagon and had hit the curb instead. I just lay on the cement for a while, groggy, until I was sure I could get up. A small group of people had collected, mostly kids, and a man helped me to my feet.

"You okay?" he asked.

"Yeah," I said, "I think so."

My knees hurt and my arms hurt and I think my *teeth* even hurt, but I could see that I wasn't bleeding anywhere, so I—

No blood.

My head was swimming, and there were kids and grown-ups all around me asking questions left and right, but the words "no blood" were like jackhammers inside my brain, pounding so hard that I had to pay attention to them and to nothing else. No blood, *no blood, NO BLOOD!*

Caesar was struck by a convertible on Berkshire, Sam had said, and before he died he had bled all over the place. Those were Sam's own words.

I picked up my shovel, pushed through the crowd of onlookers, got on my bicycle, and rode back to the vacant field at the corner of Berkshire and Hoover. As I rode, I glanced down at my badly skinned arms. The pain had died down to a steady throbbing, and small flecks of red oozed out at several spots.

Blood.

Caesar was hit by a car and had bled all over the place.

But when I got to Berkshire, there was no blood on the street, no blood on the sidewalk, no blood anywhere.

Blood! *That's* what had been missing!

But why?

The street cleaners only came by early in the morning. And what about the sidewalk? And the field itself? Who could have cleaned Caesar's blood from the *field*? And why?

Then slowly, piece by piece, the puzzle fitted itself together inside my head. Caesar killed, no blood, body stolen...

I rode over to Sam's house and, leaving my bike in the driveway, carried my shovel into the back yard.

I found what I was looking for in a strawberry patch in a corner of the yard. The patch had just been watered, so the soil was all a rich chocolatey-brown, but at the very rear of the patch, where no berry plants were growing, there was a small, slightly raised mound of dirt.

The mound was roughly the same size and shape as the dark spot I had dug up earlier, at the vacant field.

I started shoveling.

When I entered our office for the second time that day, I was tired, sweaty, and awfully proud of myself.

Nero was still seated in his overstuffed leather armchair, and Sam Cabot once again was sitting in one of the yellow folding chairs. When I walked, in they were discussing the relative merits of two different ways of making a peanut butter and jelly sandwich. Nero insisted that, to get the best combination of flavors, you had to spread the peanut butter on one slice of bread and the jelly on another, and then kind of *smish* the two slices together. But Sam held out for spreading both peanut butter and jelly onto the *same* slice of bread, and then putting the unspread slice on top to finish the sandwich.

I listened to the debate for a couple of minutes, until I got good and hungry. Then I smacked my lips nice and loud. Sam and Nero looked at me.

"Hi, Archie," Sam greeted me.

I stood there for a few moments, deciding whether or not to remember that he was a client.

"What's the matter, Arch?"

"Artie," I said menacingly. "My name is Artie."

Sam was startled. "S-sure," he mumbled.

"Sure what?"

"Sure, *Artie*."

"That's better," I growled.

"Are you finished, Arthur?" Nero asked politely. He called me Arthur when he wasn't mad at me but wanted people to think he was.

"Just about," I smiled. "Sir."

"Very good. Sam and I were talking about peanut butter and jelly, and I think we're about ready for a practical demonstration. Have you eaten?"

"That can wait," I said. "First, I'd like to report."

"Something important?"

"You could call it that. I've solved the case."

"*This* case?" he asked, nodding toward Sam Cabot.

"Right."

"Well, then," Nero smiled, "you'd better go ahead and report. Verbatim."

"What verbatim?" I scowled. "I haven't said two words to anybody all day! I just rode around! Now do you want me to report or not?"

"Certainly, Artie. Go right ahead."

"Okay," I said. And I told Nero and Sam how I'd gone to the field and dug up the empty grave, and how I'd *known* there was something missing besides the dead dachshund but couldn't pin down what it was. Then I told them how I'd suddenly realized that what had been missing at the vacant field was—

"Blood," Nero interrupted.

"Huh?" I said.

"That's what was missing. There should have been Caesar's blood all over the place, but there wasn't."

"When were you there?" I demanded.

"I haven't been out of this chair all day, Artie."

"Sam told you, then!"

"Sam told me nothing," he said smugly. "I told Sam, and he admitted I was right."

"Well, then, how did you—?"

"Proceed, Artie."

I didn't feel nearly so proud of myself anymore. If Nero hadn't left his chair at all, and Sam hadn't told him anything, how did he—?

"There wasn't any blood on Berkshire, or on the sidewalk, or on the field," I said, "so I just thought about it until I figured it out. It was pretty simple, really. The obvious thing for me to do was to grab my shovel and—"

"—and go to Sam's house."

"There's no way you can know I did that, Nero!" I exploded.

"I don't *know* what you did, Artie. I *assume* that you went over to Sam Cabot's because that's what *I* would have done if I'd been in your place. The fact that I'm right and you *did* go there doesn't make me a mind reader. It just confirms my opinion that you've got brains."

"All right," I said. "I went over to Sam's and went into the backyard, and suppose you tell me what I found in the strawberry patch?"

"Now, you see," Nero said patiently, "there are *some* things I haven't been able to figure out by myself. I know you dug a hole in Sam's back yard, but the fact that you dug it in a strawberry patch is news to me. How did you know just where to dig? Different-colored dirt again?"

"No, the whole patch had just been watered. I—"

"Ah, then you must have come across a small mound of earth and guessed that was the spot. Correct?"

"Yeah, great. I dug there, about three feet down, and found—"

"Caesar's body."

"Caesar's body. Will you let me finish one sentence, Nero, just *one*?"

"I'm sorry, Artie. Go on."

"Caesar's hair was all matted and sticky from dried blood," I said. "He smelled like lemonade, and there was a note pinned to his left ear reading, 'I wish you'd keep your crummy dog off of my field. He keeps bleeding on the crabgrass.'"

Nero blinked his large hazel eyes.

"The note," I continued, "was signed, 'Love and kisses, the Phantom of the Opera.' And the whole thing was written in green ink. In *your* handwriting."

Nero blinked again.

I swallowed, hard.

"All right, Nero," I said. "I give up. I found Caesar's body, tags and all. He was dead, but he looked perfectly okay. No blood, no note, no nothing."

"I'd already figured out that was the case, Artie," Nero murmured.

"Yeah, I bet you did. Now tell me how you did it, and then tell me what it's all supposed to mean, if you're so smart."

"*How* is easy. *What*'s a little harder, but I'm sure you've worked most of it out for yourself. After you left for the vacant field this afternoon, I just sat here and thought about the case. I wasn't satisfied with our conclusion that the hit-and-run driver had stolen Caesar's body to avoid being identified. The more I thought about that possibility, the less sense it made.

"But it still seemed obvious that the body was stolen because there was something wrong with it, something that *someone* didn't want us to see."

"What could be wrong?"

"Well, the only thing I knew about Caesar's body was that it had been struck by a car and there was lots of blood. What could be wrong with *that*?

"And then the whole thing came rushing at me like a swimming pool does after you've jumped off the high diving board. *Smack*! I had it! We weren't supposed to see the body because there *wasn't* any blood on it! Once we saw it, we'd know that Caesar hadn't been hit by a car at all.

"So Sam had lied about the car, lied about the blood—in fact, Sam had even lied about burying Caesar in the vacant field. Caesar's body wasn't stolen from the field—*it was never there to begin with!*

"Once I'd worked all of this out, I called my brother Perry in and asked him to go get Sam. When Sam got here, I told him I knew his story was a pack of lies and demanded that he tell me the truth. Sam, tell Artie what you told me."

"I—I'm sorry it worked out this way, Ar-*Artie*," Sam began, "but Nero's right. You see, I was playing with my chemistry set this morning and I mixed a lot of the things together—calcium carbonate, tannic acid, all kinds of chemicals. Then I decided to do an experiment and feed the mixture to Caesar. I didn't think anything would happen! I just stirred it into his water dish and watched him lap it up. He seemed to really like it."

Sam wiped the back of his hand across his sunburnt nose and sniffled.

"Nothing much happened for a few minutes," he continued, "but then Caesar started to whine, like. I tried to get him to stop, but he kept whining and moaning and everything, and finally he just lay down and closed his eyes and started shivering.

"In a little while, he stopped shivering. I felt for his heartbeat, but it was gone. I'd killed him.

"I was scared, Artie, real scared! Then I thought about telling everyone a car hit him and killed him. If I made up a description of some out-of-state car, I figured everybody would look for it for a while and then give up and forget all about it.

"But I realized that, when you saw Caesar, you'd know no car had hit him because there wasn't any blood. And I knew I couldn't hit him myself and make him bleed—I just couldn't hit Caesar."

"But you gave him that junk from the chemistry set," I said, disgusted.

"I didn't think it would hurt him! It's not the same thing, don't you understand?"

Sam's small skinny frame started quivering, and I turned away. I don't like to see fellows cry, and I wasn't feeling any too sympathetic toward Sam in the first place.

"All *right*," I said. "So it was an accident. What happened next?"

Sam kept on sobbing.

"Nero?" I said.

"I accused Sam of killing Caesar in a way that left no visible marks. He then told me about the chemistry set. But, you see, I had already deduced—"

"I *believe* you!" I shouted. "Just tell me what happened!"

"Well," Nero *harrumphed*, "let me see. Sam buried his dog in his back yard, then went to the vacant field at Berkshire and Hoover and dug a hole. When he had filled in the hole, he noticed the difference in color between where he'd dug and the dirt all around, so he went home and watered down the strawberry patch, just to play it safe. He didn't want anyone noticing that someone had been digging in his back yard, not with Caesar's body supposedly missing. But he didn't notice that the dirt was a little higher where he had buried Caesar than anywhere else. And then he came to us with his story."

"And by the time I finally realized that no blood on Berkshire meant that Caesar hadn't been run over and found the body and figured that *Sam* had killed him, you'd already doped it all out. So what do we do now, Chief?"

"Well, Artie, Caesar's death *was* an accident, and you can see how badly Sam feels about it. I told him we'd keep our mouths shut and help spread the story of a hit-and-run. It'll keep Sam out of trouble."

"You mean we play it like we couldn't find the killer?"

"Right. And since our taking money for keeping quiet sounds too much like blackmail, I've given back Sam's retainer.

"Now, as I said before, when you got here Sam and I were about to test our theories about how to make a peanut butter and jelly sandwich, and I...."

*

So Nero Wolfe had solved the case, refused payment, let the criminal off, and was now getting ready to *feed* him. All without lifting his slightly pudgy ninety-five pounds from his chair. And what did I have to show for it? A wasted afternoon, dirty clothes, and a lot of bruises.

I sighed—and went to the kitchen to fetch peanut butter, jelly, and bread.

One last thing.

Our ruse worked real good, and pretty soon people stopped looking for the nonexistent off-white convertible. Sam's parents even bought him another dachshund, a female this time, which Sam named Cleopatra.

And when Cleo had pups, months later, I strolled into our office one afternoon after school to find Nero playing with the pride of the litter.

"Sam give you that?" I asked.

"Yes. As a token of his thanks."

"What are you going to call it?"

"Him," Nero corrected. "I can't decide."

"How about Fido?"

"How about shutting up? I want his name to have something to do with what he looks like. Like you'd call a spotted dog Spot or a red one Red."

I looked at Cleo's pride. It—I mean *he*—was a small, dark-brown, very fat puppy.

"How about Fat Fido?" I suggested.

"Artie."

"Plump Prince?" I asked meekly.

"Pfui," Nero Wolfe replied.

"Hey, I've got it! Call him Stout Rex," I said, and ran for cover.

50

originally published in *Ellery Queen's Mystery Magazine* (November/December 2018)

INTRODUCTION BY JANET HUTCHINGS:

Fifty years ago this month, Josh Pachter appeared in EQMM's "Department of First Stories," while still a teenager! In the intervening years he's authored more than sixty stories, many of them collaborations with other authors—making him one of the most successful literary collaborators in our genre. He's also one of mystery's foremost translators.

The leaves outside his office window had burned, almost without his notice, from green to gold to gone. There were a few stragglers, he saw now, few enough to count.

Professor Griffen found that he was counting them, realized what he was doing and forced himself to drag his eyes away from the window and back to his computer. From the speakers on either side of the monitor, James Taylor sang about fire and rain, and the coincidence reminded him that he was supposed to be updating his lecture notes on Robert Frost for a generation of students—a giggle of girls, a bluster of boys—whose mental temperature had devolved into such lukewarmth he despaired of ever convincing them that fire and ice were momentous enough to even momentarily divert their attention from their Instagrams and Twitter feeds.

There were fewer words on his screen than leaves on the trees, and he felt himself no more capable of adding to the former tally than to the latter.

"Thought I'd see you, thought I'd see you, fire and rain, now...."

James Taylor's voice faded away, was replaced by "Fifty Years After the Fair," and not for the first time he marveled at iTunes' telepathic ability to follow—or lead?—his thoughts.

How, he wondered, could he possibly capture the interest of the teenagers in his freshman lit class? He'd been a teenager himself, once upon a time—but it was fifty years after *that* fair. Half a century ago, his widowed father and three siblings had clustered around the nineteen-inch television in the family room to listen to Walter Cronkite tell them about Vietnam on the evening news. Today, with their screens in their pockets and five hundred channels to choose from, all his students seemed to know or care about was which Kardashian was having sex with which football player or rapper....

"Fifty years after the fair," Aimee Mann sang, "I drink from a different cup. But it does no good to compare, 'cause nothing ever measures up."

He turned away again, away from both monitor and window, and let his gaze drift across the spines of his dearest friends, his books, the fat poetry anthologies and slender chapbooks and single-author collections he had accumulated over the course of his career.

Perhaps it was the song that steered his fingers to the line-up of old magazines on the bookcase's bottom shelf. There were several dozen of them, long-ignored souvenirs of his youth. He slid the left-most volume free and held it in his hands, surprised to see how well the green and red and yellow cover had withstood the passing of five decades.

"Nine NEW stories," the bold red letters beneath the yellow words that identified the publication proudly announced. He counted only six writers listed on the cover—Hugh Pentecost, Lawrence Treat, Agatha Christie, Berkely Mather, Celia Fremlin, George Harmon Coxe—then gingerly opened the old magazine and smiled to see his own name included in the table of contents.

A folded sheet of paper tucked between the pages marked the location of his contribution. He'd long since forgotten that editor Frederic Dannay—who, with his cousin Manfred B. Lee, had written those marvelous novels and short stories, beginning way back in the late 1920s—had devoted an entire page of the magazine, page 106, to an introduction.

"Department of First Stories," he read. "This is the 325th 'first story' to be published by *Ellery Queen's Mystery Magazine* ... another 'first' by a teenager (God bless 'em!)...."

And then, on the facing page, the title and byline: "E.Q. GRIFFEN EARNS HIS NAME, by Ellery Queen Griffen."

He sat there, completely absorbed, for fifteen minutes, rereading the story for the first time in—how long?—certainly thirty years, probably forty. It wasn't bad, really, was actually rather *good* for the sixteen-year-old he'd been when he wrote it, especially if he compared it to the drivel produced by the majority of his current students, who were two or three years older than he'd been when he'd written it back in 1968.

The professor's father, Ross Griffen, a homicide detective with the Tyson County Police Department, had been a lifelong fan of detective fiction, and he'd somehow convinced his wife to allow him to name their four children after the heroes—and one heroine—of his literary passion. Sherlock Holmes Griffen, Jane Marple Griffen, Ellery Queen Griffen, and Nero Wolfe Griffen. For the purposes of this, his first short story, young Ellery had expanded the family to *eleven* children, adding siblings named Peter Wimsey, Albert Campion, Parker Pyne, Perry Mason, Augustus Van Dusen, Gideon Fell, and John Jericho to the brood.

For his debut outing, the real E.Q. Griffen had provided his fictional namesake with two invented mysteries to solve, a trivial neighborhood case of some stolen apple pies, and a dying-message murder brought home to the dinner table by the Griffens' paterfamilias. And the fictional E.Q. Griffen had solved the murder by employing an Ellery Queen-like combination of deductive reasoning plus a flash of inspiration—thus "earning his name" in the parlance of the make-believe family he had based on his actual family—while completely failing to solve the case of the missing pies.

Cute. Of course, his first and middle names and age had been what had caught Fred Dannay's eye. But the story itself had a certain charm, the professor thought now. He wondered why he'd added only seven extra boys to the family, when one more would have resulted in an even dozen, which ought to have been much more satisfying to his mathematically inclined brain. He wondered also why neither he nor Fred Dannay had noticed the anachronism of naming one of the invented children after Hugh Pentecost's John Jericho, a character who hadn't been created until the middle Sixties and thus couldn't possibly have been a favorite from Ross Griffen's childhood.

According to Fred Dannay's introduction, Ellery had already "roughed out" plots for Gideon Fell Griffen and Augie Van Dusen Griffen stories by the time this first one appeared in print. He couldn't remember ever having actually *written* those, though perhaps he had and Mr. Dannay had rejected them. There *had* in fact been a couple of sequels—"E.Q. Griffen's Second Case" in 1970, and "Sam Buried Caesar," featuring Nero Wolfe Griffen, in '71—but after that he'd moved on to creating fiction *not* about his imaginary self and siblings, one or two stories a year until the birth of his daughter in 1986, then fewer until she was grown and flown, then more again thereafter.

The professor noted that, in yet another instance of iTunes mind meld, his speakers had segued into Bruce Springsteen's "Born in the U.S.A."

"I'm ten years burning down the road. Nowhere to run, ain't got nowhere to go...."

No, he wasn't ready to think another decade into the future. In ten years, he would be seventy-six, an old man, his roads, his bridges, burned. Now, at "only" sixty-six, he could still delude himself into thinking of himself as middle-aged.

He sighed, absently retrieved the folded bookmark from his desk and began to return it to its place, but found his curiosity piqued and unfolded it.

It was a photocopy of a sheet of ordinary lined notebook paper, and in the center of the page was the number 50 in large sprawling numerals.

He blinked at the odd coincidence, then suddenly recalled what that faded piece of paper *was*, and the walls of his office and the leaves on the trees and the last half century of his life dissolved into nothingness, leaving him immersed in a memory he had long since left behind....

*

"Of course, not all mysteries are crimes," Ross Griffen said, reaching for another slice of pizza. Contributor's copies of the December 1968 issue of EQMM had arrived in that afternoon's mail, and the inspector had taken the family out for everyone's favorite dinner to celebrate. "Examples, please?"

"Stonehenge," said Sherlock, whose knowledge of the geography of the British Isles was as sharp as his namesake's, if not sharper.

"How the Egyptians built the pyramids," Nero added, studiously picking pepperoni off his own second slice.

"The disappearance of Amelia Earhart," said Jane.

"That one might *have been a crime," Ellery pointed out. "Someone might have sabotaged her plane, or her navigator—Ed Noonan?—might have—"*

*"*Fred *Noonan," their father put in.*

"—Fred Noonan," Ellery went on, "might have killed her."

"Possible," the inspector conceded. "But the point I want to make is that not all crimes are mysteries, either—and I have an example from right here in Tyson County."

The four kids scootched their chairs closer to the round table and fixed their attention on their father, who they knew was about to share a new case with them—something the four of them loved even more than they loved pizza.

"Solomon Kaine," the inspector began, "was a nationally known military historian specializing in the armies of the Roman Empire and a full professor and chair of the history department at an Ivy League university. About five years ago, though, when his wife, Abby, died of cancer in her early forties, Kaine gave up his tenure and moved here with their two children—Solomon, Junior and Romy—to take a much less visible job teaching Western Civ at Tyson County Community College. He's been here ever since, and you probably know his kids, they both go to your school. Solomon, Junior's a senior—"

"He's president of the Student Council," Sherlock cut in, "and a really cool guy, always ready to help you with your homework, if you're having trouble understanding how to do it."

"Everybody calls him Solo, because he sings in the choir," added Jane dreamily. "He has a gorgeous *voice. Tenor, clear as a bell."*

"—and Romy's a junior," the inspector went on, "a year ahead of

you, Ellery. Do you know her?"

"Not well. She's pretty quiet, keeps to herself mostly. If she's got friends, I don't know who they are."

"I've heard people say," said Jane, all seriousness now, "that her father's been, well, molesting her. I don't know if there's any truth to it or not, it's just rumors."

Inspector Griffen leaned back in his chair and folded his arms across his chest. "Apparently it is true," he said, "or at least it was, but Professor Kaine will never molest his daughter—or anyone else—again. He's dead."

Nero, the youngest, looked up sharply. "Dead?"

The inspector nodded. "Solomon, Junior called the station about eleven-fifteen last night. His sister had finally told him about their father's ... well, let's say 'actions,' and Solo confronted him. Solomon, Senior basically told him to mind his own business, and Solo said he just lost it, picked up a letter opener from his father's desk and stabbed him in the chest with it."

"No," Jane whispered, horrified.

"I'm afraid so. Solo ran off, but then he realized that he had to take responsibility for what he'd done, and he found a pay phone and called that new 9-1-1 number. He was waiting outside the house when the squad cars got there, and he let us in and took us back to his father's study."

"Where you found Solomon, Senior, dead," said Nero flatly.

"Correct, slumped over his desk. As it turns out, though, Senior hadn't died right away. After Solo stabbed him and ran, he lived long enough to pick up a pen and begin to write his son's name."

The inspector took a folded piece of paper from his pocket, unfolded it, and shoved the metal pizza tray aside to make room for it in the center of the table. It was a photocopy of a sheet of ordinary lined notebook paper, and in the center of the page were the letters S-O in large sprawling capitals.

"Solo," Ellery said slowly.

"Or Solomon," his father amended. "Or Solomon, Junior. In any case, he was identifying his son as his killer, but he died before he could finish writing. Which turns out to be irrelevant, since Solo freely confessed to the crime."

"Where is he now?" asked Sherlock.

The inspector sighed. "In a holding cell at headquarters. He'll sit there until his trial."

"They won't let him out on bail?" said Jane.

"Probably not, honey. He'll be charged with second-degree murder, and I think the judge is unlikely to agree to bail. Even if he does, he'll set it so high that there's no way Solo will be able to bond out. I'm afraid he'll stay in jail until—well, until he goes to prison."

"A crime but not a mystery," Ellery said slowly. "Q.E.D."

The professor blinked his eyes and returned to the present.

His father's prediction, he remembered, had been correct. Solo Kaine had been charged with murder in the second degree, the district attorney had agreed to let him plead down to manslaughter, and the teenager had been sentenced to ten years.

Which meant, he realized, that in principle Solo had been back out in the world for the last four decades.

He found himself wondering what had happened to the boy—now, of course, a boy no longer but a man of almost seventy. Had he put his incarceration behind him and managed to make something of the rest of his life, or had prison destroyed his future, as it destroyed the futures of so many young men, not just the career criminals but also those whose otherwise quiet lives had been ruined by a single error in judgment, a single momentary loss of reason and control?

He swiveled decisively back to his monitor, poised his fingers above his keyboard for a moment, and began to type.

A search on "Solomon Kaine" (without the quotation marks) produced almost half a million hits in 0.86 seconds, and Ellery was confused by what showed up on his screen until he realized—after considerably longer than eight-tenths of a second—that Google had auto-corrected his accurate spelling to the in-this-case-inaccurate "Solomon Kane," which turned out to be the title of a 2009 fantasy film, based on a comic-book hero and starring a roster of people he'd never heard of ... along with, oddly, Max von Sydow, who he'd thought was long dead.

Clicking on "did you mean: solomon *kaine*" took another half a second and delivered just over a hundred thousand hits. He scrolled down the first page and found links to reviews of several of Kaine, Senior's books—most of which were long out of print, but one, a text on the Punic Wars, was still available on Amazon and apparently in use at a number of universities—and, near the bottom of the page, an obituary from the *Tyson Times*, dated November 21, 1968.

Rather than read the obit, the professor launched a new search, this time on "Solomon Kaine, Junior" (*with* the quotation marks). In an even smaller fraction of a second, he was presented with under a thousand hits, beginning with news stories about the murder and Solo's subsequent plea bargain and sentencing ... and then this headline jumped out at him: "YOUTH, 20, KILLED IN PRISON ATTACK."

Ellery's heart stopped.

Dreading what he would find, he clicked on the link and read the story.

And, yes, poor Solo, in the second year of his ten-year sentence, had tried to intervene when a group of older convicts ganged up on a newly incarcerated felon at the state penitentiary, and had himself been stabbed in the stomach with a shank that had been filed down from the grip end of a plastic toothbrush. He had died of his wounds in the prison hospital, without regaining consciousness. The inmate he had been trying to save had also been killed in the incident.

Dead at twenty. What a tragic end to a tragic story.

Or *was* it the end of the story?

Once upon a time, criminal investigation had meant legwork, had meant visiting newspaper morgues and libraries and police departments and victims' and witnesses' and suspects' homes and offices in person. But now, in 2018, the phrase "armchair detective" had taken on new meaning, and there was practically no limit to what you could learn, simply by letting your fingers do the walking.

Ellery did a search on "Romy Kaine" and came up completely empty. Of course, the girl had probably gotten married and taken her husband's last name—and he recalled vaguely that "Romy" was a nickname, anyway, short for something else, like "Solo" was short for "Solomon."

Romany? Romanette? He couldn't recall. It was an unusual name, he thought, but he couldn't put his finger on it. Had he ever even known what it was?

Romanov? Romula? Romaine?

The only other Romy he'd ever heard of was Romy Schneider, the actress, so he looked *her* up and found that she'd been born Rosemarie Magdalena Albach.

He tried "Rosemarie Magdalena Kaine" and then "Rosemarie Kaine," thinking Solomon, Senior or his wife might perhaps have been a fan.

Nothing.

And then—cursing himself for resorting to the notorious user-editable website he constantly cautioned his students to avoid—he backtracked to Romy Schneider's Wikipedia page and learned that she hadn't made her film debut until 1953, when, at the tender age of fifteen, she'd appeared in a German picture titled *Wenn der Weisse Flieder wieder blüht.*

So Romy Kaine—who was a year older than Ellery, who had himself been born in 1951—couldn't possibly have been named after the actress.

And then he cursed himself again for his slowness on the uptake and went back to the very first search page he'd consulted and clicked on Solomon Senior's obituary.

And there it was: "Survived by his son, Solomon Kaine, Junior, and daughter, Romanelle Kaine."

Romanelle.

Now that he saw the name in black and white on the screen, he felt certain he had *not* ever heard it before. To him, she had always been just Romy.

He searched on "Romanelle Kaine," and there *she* was, almost instantly: Romanelle Kaine Washington. So she *had* married, after all, and had indeed taken her husband's name.

And she—like her mother and father and brother before her—was also dead. She had died on February 23, 2015, according to her obituary, just before her sixty-fifth birthday, of lung cancer, leaving behind a devoted husband, Richard Washington, three grown children—two daughters and a son—and five loving grandchildren.

Lung cancer. Ellery wondered if she had been a smoker.

He picked up his faded bookmark and refolded it and reached for the magazine in which he'd rediscovered it to put it back where, after all this time, it seemed to belong.

And then he froze.

He unfolded the sheet of paper and stared at it—and asked himself a question he ought to have asked fifty years ago, a question he *hadn't* asked, a question *no one* had thought to ask at the time.

If Solomon Kaine, Senior, had meant to identify his son as his killer, then why had he begun to write the word SOLOMON in the *center* of a sheet of paper? Why hadn't he begun writing further to the left on the page?

Stop it, he told himself. *Not every crime is a mystery.*

The man had been stabbed with a letter opener, for Pete's sake. He was *dying.* To give him credit for having the presence of mind to pay the slightest attention to the positioning of his message on the page would be a stretch, the sort of minutiae that Ellery's namesake might well have integrated into one of his dying-message short stories or novels.

In the real world, though, the man would surely have grabbed a pen and begun to scrawl, without any thought whatsoever as to *where* he was scrawling.

But still...

The possibility nagged at him, and he felt that it connected to something else, to some nebulous factor that tickled the darkest corner of his mind.

What, he asked himself, if the letters S-O weren't *part* of the victim's final message but the entire thing, perfectly centered on the page?

S-O.

So.

So.

So *what?*

And then Ellery realized what it was that was bothering him.

When he had first drawn the old photocopy from its resting place and unfolded it, he had been thinking about the fiftieth anniversary of his first publication and had, thanks to the power of suggestion, seen the markings in the middle of the page as the numbers 5 and 0, and only a moment later remembered that they were instead the letters S and O.

What if, fifty years ago, the exact same thing had happened—but in reverse? When the police had been called out to the Kaine residence, had moved the dead man's body and found his dying message beneath it, they had been thinking about Solomon Kaine, both the father who was dead and the son who had confessed to his murder. So they had quite naturally seen the markings as an S and an O, the first letters of the supposed killer's name.

But what if the dying man had in fact written the numbers 5 and 0, after all? What if he had written exactly what he had been *trying* to write: the number 50?

Fifty.

What would have been the significance of *that* in the mind of a dying man?

Most Americans worked fifty weeks a year, devoting only two weeks to vacation.

He shook his head.

There were fifty states in the Union, had been for almost a decade by 1968, since Hawaii had become the fiftieth in 1959—and it must have been around 1968, Ellery thought, that the television series *Hawaii Five-O* had debuted.

Five-O?

He snorted in irritation.

His fingers flew over his keyboard, and Google told him that there are Fifty Gates of Wisdom in the Kabbalah, that fifty is the atomic number of tin, that fifty is the smallest number that can be produced in two different ways by adding together two non-zero squares: $1^2 + 7^2$ and $5^2 + 5^2$.

He gritted his teeth.

Ridiculous. The same sort of incongruous foolishness the fictional Ellery Queen had so often considered and rejected in his own dying-message fiction.

Fifty.

Fifty.

"Are you reelin' in the years," Steely Dan asked from his speakers, "stowin' away the time? Are you gatherin' up the tears? Have you had enough of mine?"

Reelin' in the years, he thought. *Fifty years after the fair.*

Years.

And then he remembered that Solomon, Senior had been a historian, a specialist in ancient Roman military history, the author of a book on the Punic Wars.

He Googled, felt momentarily hopeful when he saw that there had been *three* Punic Wars between Rome and Carthage, then swore aloud to see that the first of them had begun in 264 BC and the last had ended with the obliteration of Carthage in 146 BC.

So, *not* the Punic Wars.

He searched on 50 BC and found that it was the year the Roman Republic had annexed Judea ... and approximately the year in which the Asterix comic books were set.

In 50 AD, the Dutch city of Utrecht was founded, and Cai Lun, the Chinese inventor of paper, was born. And Solomon Kaine's message had been written on—

Ellery wished he had more hair, so he could rip it out in frustration.

Fifty.

Fifty *years*...

Of course, 50 BC and 50 AD weren't the *only* years containing the number 50.

In 1750, Mozart's rival Antonio Salieri was born and Johann Sebastian Bach died.

In 1850, Nathaniel Hawthorne's *The Scarlet Letter*—a book he had taught his American Lit students dozens of times—was published, California became the thirty-first state, and the Pinkerton National Detective Agency was founded.

In 1950, the year before Ellery was born, Alger Hiss was sentenced to prison for perjury, Harry Truman ordered the development of the hydrogen bomb, and the Korean War began.

The Korean War.

And Solomon, Senior was a military hist—

And then, all at once, fifty puzzle pieces fitted neatly together in that part of the professor's brain where inspiration lurked.

Rumor had it that Solomon Kaine had been abusing his daughter Romy.

Romy Kaine had died in February of 2015, just before her sixty-fifth birthday, which meant she had been born in 1950, the year before Ellery.

Which fit, because Ellery had been born in '51, and Romy was a year ahead of him in school.

And Solomon Senior was a historian, a specialist in the armies of ancient Rome.

Who had named his daughter Romanelle.

Roman L.

In Roman numerals, L = 50.

And Romy Kaine was born in 1950.

Ellery drew a deep breath and let it out.

In 1968, when Solomon, Senior was killed, his daughter Romy was eighteen. What if *she* was the one who had plunged that letter opener into her father's chest? What if *she* had run off, not realizing that he was not yet dead? What if she had found her older brother and told him what she had done, and he—*a really cool guy*, Sherlock had called him, *always ready to help*, surely fiercely protective of his kid sister—had convinced her to let *him* take the blame for her desperate act?

What if he had gone into his father's study, had wiped Romy's prints from the letter opener and carefully replaced them with his own, had called the police to confess to the crime ... all without realizing that his dying father had named Romy as his killer, leaving hidden beneath his body a message the police, with Solo's confession at hand, had misunderstood?

For fifty years, the world had thought of Solo Kaine as a murderer. Now he, E.Q. Griffen, could set the record straight.

Or could he?

There was no way to *prove*, at this late date, what had really happened that night, half a century ago.

But at least he could offer a logical alternative explanation for the "facts" of the case that had been accepted for all these years, could show that perhaps young Solo had been nothing worse than a loving big brother who had made the ultimate sacrifice for the sake of his sister.

And then what?

What would the revelation of that possibility do to Richard Washington, to Romy's children and grandchildren?

Ellery remembered a scrap of Latin he'd seen often in the Golden Age detective novels he'd been raised on.

Cui bono?

Who benefits?

Surely Solomon, Senior could have taught him the original historical importance of that phrase, could have cited chapter and verse.

But Solomon, Senior was dead.

And so was Solo, and so was Romy.

While Richard Washington and his descendants were—at least as of the publication of Romy's obituary in 2015—still alive.

Who would it benefit to tell them that their wife, their mother, their grandmother, was perhaps a murderess, no matter how understandable the horrible circumstances that had led her to her one moment of violence?

Ellery sat there at his desk for a long time, the sheet of paper in his hand, his eyes closed, his lips pursing slightly in and out—a habit he'd picked up from his brother Nero and had never lost.

Fifty years ago, at the ripe old age of sixteen, he'd thought of himself as an invincible crime buster, a Master Detective, all-knowing, able to leap tall mysteries in a single mental bound.

But *not all crimes are mysteries,* his father had cautioned him, using the case of the Solomon Kaines, *père et fils,* to make his point. And, he realized now, it had been that bursting of his poetic belief that law enforcement in real life was all about the unraveling of riddles, as it was in his beloved books, that had led Ellery to abandon his idea of becoming a policeman like his father and turn, like Citizen Kaine, to academia.

And now, fifty years after the fair, with the end of his journey almost visible through the mist and much closer to where he sat than its beginning, he saw himself for what he was: flawed, and limited, and every bit as capable of error as of wisdom.

But the law is the law, he told himself, *even fifty years on. If not for the law, society crumbles and chaos reigns.*

But which is the greater good, he asked himself, *to uphold the law, or to be a human being? Which is more important: being right, or being merciful?*

"Truth will come to light," Shakespeare's Launcelot had declaimed in *The Merchant of Venice*; "murder can not be hid long."

"Then you will know the truth," said Jesus in *The Gospel of John*, "and the truth shall set you free."

But what if the truth accomplished nothing of value, set no one free, and caused nothing but pain?

Was it better to tell a painful truth, or to let sleeping dogs lie?

Righteousness? Or mercy?

Ice? Or fire?

Which brought him back to Robert Frost.

The professor sighed, refolded the sheet of paper yet again, slipped it back into the pages of *Ellery Queen's Mystery Magazine* and slid the issue into its accustomed place at the far left end of the bottom shelf of his bookcase.

And then he swiveled back to his computer and resumed preparing his notes for tomorrow's lecture.

ACKNOWLEDGMENTS

Many people provided invaluable assistance in the preparation of this book. I thank them, one and all, especially:

Richard Dannay, Joshua Bilmes of the Jabberwocky Literary Agency, and the trustees of the Frederic Dannay Literary Property Trust and the Manfred B. Lee Family Literary Property Trust for permission to use the Ellery Queen characters and the original five Puzzle Club stories.

Richard Dannay again, plus Dale Andrews, Jon Breen, Martin Edwards, Joe Goodrich, Janet Hutchings, Jeff Marks, Mike Nevins, Kurt Sercu, and Arthur Vidro for contributing thoughtful introductions to the ten Puzzle Club stories collected in these pages.

High marks to Jeff Marks again, for providing copies of two of the original Puzzle Club stories I was unable to track down elsewhere.

I'm grateful to Janet Hutchings, the editor of *Ellery Queen's Mystery Magazine*, for buying my Puzzle Club pastiches for *EQMM*, and to Jackie Sherbow, Carol Demont, and the folks at Dell Magazines and Penny Press for their support and encouragement over the years.

Kudos, of course, to Jeff Marks and Douglas Greene at Crippen & Landru for shepherding *The Puzzle Club* from a glimmer of an idea into the book you now hold in your hands.

And, most of all, my eternal gratitude to Frederic Dannay and Manfred B. Lee, whose creation of Ellery Queen in 1929 and of the Puzzle Club in 1965 made this volume possible.

Josh Pachter
July 2022

The Adventures of the Puzzle Club And Other Stories

The Adventures of the Puzzle Club And Other Stories by Ellery Queen and Josh Pachter is printed on 60 pound paper, and is designed by Jeffrey Marks using InDesign. The type is Jenson, an old-style serif typeface based on text by Nicolas Jenson in the late Fifteenth Century. The printing and binding is by Southern Ohio Printing for the clothbound pages and cover and the trade paperback edition. Clothbound book binding is from Cincinnati Bindery. The book was published in October 2022 by Crippen & Landru Publishers, Inc., Cincinnati, OH.

COPYRIGHT INFORMATION

ABOUT THE CONTRIBUTORS

DALE C. ANDREWS (1949–) is a lifelong Ellery Queen fan, the author of four Ellery Queen pastiches (all of which were originally published in *Ellery Queen's Mystery Magazine*), and the co-editor of *The Misadventures of Ellery Queen* (Wildside Press, 2018) and *The Further Misadventures of Ellery Queen* (Wildside Press, 2020). He has been a regular contributor at *SleuthSayers*, the mystery short story writers' blog, and a guest contributor at *Something Is Going to Happen*, the *EQMM* mystery blog. He previously was the Deputy Assistant General Counsel for Litigation at the U.S. Department of Transportation and an adjunct professor at the University of Denver.

JON L. BREEN (1943–) is the author of eight novels (two of which were shortlisted for CWA Dagger Awards), over one hundred short stories, and two Edgar-winning reference books (*What About Murder: A Guide to Books About Mystery and Detective Fiction* and *Novel Verdicts: A Guide to Courtroom Fiction*). His first story, a parody of Ed McBain's 87th Precinct books, appeared in *EQMM* in 1967, and he wrote *EQMM*'s "Jury Box" book-review column for about thirty years. His critical work also appears in *Mystery Scene.*

FREDERIC DANNAY (1905–1982) was one half of the legendary "Ellery Queen" writing team. Starting with *The Roman Hat Mystery* in 1929, he and his first cousin Manfred B. Lee produced some three dozen novels and dozens of short stories over the next forty years, ending with *A Fine and Private Place* in 1971. Dannay is also remembered as an anthologist, a scholar, a collector of rare books … and as the founder and first editor-in-chief of *EQMM.*

RICHARD DANNAY (1939–), one of Frederic Dannay's sons, is a New York City lawyer and litigator specializing in copyright and publishing law. His copyright cases have involved matters such as John Steinbeck's works, the novel and movie *Jurassic Park*, Dorothy Parker's poems, and Grateful Dead concert posters. He has published articles on copyright law's controversial "fair use" doctrine, and is a past president of the Copyright Society of the USA. He's also a book collector and member of the Grolier Club.

MARTIN EDWARDS (1955–) is the author of twenty crime novels, including the Harry Devlin, Lake District, and Rachel Savernake series. He has written many short stories for *EQMM* and anthologies. His non-fiction books include *The Golden Age of Murder* and *The Life of Crime: Detecting the History of Mysteries and Their Creators*, a history of the genre. He is a former Chair of the Crime Writers' Association, consultant to the British Library's Crime Classics, and current president of the Detection Club. He has received the CWA Diamond Dagger, Short Story Dagger, and Dagger in the Library awards, plus other honors including an Edgar, an Agatha, and two Macavitys.

JOSEPH GOODRICH (1963–) is a playwright and author. His adaptation of Ellery Queen's *Calamity Town* received the 2016 Calgary Theater Critics' Award for Best New Script. His adaptations of *The Red Box* and *Might As Well Be Dead* marked Nero Wolfe's stage debut, and *Panic* won the 2008 Edgar for Best Play. He is the editor of *Blood Relations: The Selected Letters of Ellery Queen, 1947-1950* and *People in a Magazine: The Selected Letters of S. N. Behrman and His Editors at "The New Yorker,"* and the author of *Unusual Suspects: Selected Non-Fiction.* His short stories have appeared in *EQMM*, *AHMM*, and two Mystery Writers of America anthologies. An alumnus of New Dramatists and a former Calderwood Fellow at MacDowell, he lives in NYC.

JANET HUTCHINGS (1953–) has been the editor of *EQMM* since 1991. She was honored for her contributions to the field by the 2003 Bouchercon World Mystery Convention and is a co-recipient of the MWA's Ellery Queen Award and the Malice Domestic convention's Poirot Award. In recognition of *EQMM*'s "Passport to Crime" department, which she founded, she was honored by the New York branch of the International Association of Crime Writers. Her own EQ pastiche, "Change of Scene" (in which Ellery's "girl Friday" Nicki Porter takes center stage) appeared in *The Further Misadventures of Ellery Queen*.

MANFRED B. LEE (1905–1971) was one half of the legendary "Ellery Queen" writing team. Starting with *The Roman Hat Mystery* in 1929, he and his first cousin Frederic Dannay produced some three dozen novels and dozens of short stories over the next forty years, ending with *A Fine and Private Place* in 1971.

JEFFREY MARKS (1960–) is the publisher of Crippen & Landru and the author of three biographies of mystery writers: *Who Was That*

Lady? Craig Rice, the Queen of Screwball Mystery, *Atomic Renaissance*: *Women Mystery Writers of the 1940s and 1950s*, and *Anthony Boucher: A Biobibliography*. He has been nominated for an Edgar, multiple Agathas and Macavity Awards. He won the Anthony for the Boucher biography. He is currently working on a biography of the two cousins who wrote together as Ellery Queen.

Until his retirement, **FRANCIS M. NEVINS** (1943–) had a day job as a professor at the St. Louis University School of Law. Away from the lectern, he has written more than forty short stories (which have appeared in *EQMM*, *AHMM*, and other national magazines) and six mystery novels. He has also edited more than fifteen mystery anthologies and collections and is the author of several nonfiction books on the genre, two of which won Edgars from the MWA. Among his contributions to the field is *Ellery Queen: The Art of Detection* (Perfect Crime Books, 2013).

JOSH PACHTER (1951–) is a writer, editor and translator. His short fiction has appeared in *EQMM, AHMM,* and many other places. He co-edited *The Misadventures of Ellery Queen* (Wildside Press, 2018) and *The Further Misadventures of Ellery Queen* (Wildside Press, 2020) with Dale C. Andrews, and edited *The Misadventures of Nero Wolfe* (Mysterious Press, 2020), *The Man Who Read Mysteries: The Short Fiction of William Brittain* (Crippen & Landru, 2018), and *The Man Who Solved Mysteries: More Short Fiction by William Brittain* (Crippen & Landru, 2021). In 2020, he received the Short Mystery Fiction Society's Edward D. Hoch Memorial Golden Derringer Award for Lifetime Achievement.

KURT SERCU (1963-) is the founder and proprietor of *Ellery Queen—A Website on Deduction*, the most extensive EQ resource on the internet (*http://queen.spaceports.com*). He lives in Belgium, where he is the head nurse for cardiology and vascular surgery at the AZ Alma hospital in Eeklo.

ARTHUR VIDRO (1962–) wrote the introduction to T.S. Stribling's *Dr. Poggioli: Criminologist* (2004) and was the proofreader on Ellery Queen's *The Adventure of the Murdered Moths and Other Radio Mysteries* (2005); both of these books were published by Crippen & Landru. He works as a freelance editor and proofreader (mysteries a specialty) and self-publishes the thrice-yearly journal *(Give Me That) Old-Time Detection*, which explores detective fiction of the past. His mystery-fiction articles have sold to *EQMM* and *Mystery Scene*.

Crippen & Landru, Publishers
P. O. Box 532057
Cincinnati, OH 45253
Web: www.Crippenlandru.com
E-mail: Orders@crippenlandru.com

Crippen & Landru Publications

Challenge the Impossible: The Impossible Files of Dr. Sam Hawthorne by Edward D. Hoch. Full cloth in dust jacket, signed and numbered by the publisher, $45.00. Trade softcover, $19.00.

Nothing Is Impossible: Further Problems of Dr. Sam Hawthorne by Edward D. Hoch.
Dr. Sam Hawthorne, a New England country doctor in the first half of the twentieth century, was constantly faced by murders in locked rooms and impossible disappearances. *Nothing Is Impossible* contains fifteen of Dr. Sam's most extraordinary cases. Full cloth in dust jacket, signed and numbered by the publisher, $45.00. Trade softcover, $19.00.

Chain of Witnesses; The Cases of Miss Phipps by Phyllis Bentley, edited by Marvin Lachman. Lost Classics Series.
A critic writes, "stylistically, [Bentley's] stories ... share a quiet humor and misleading simplicity of statement with the works of Christie .... Her work [is] informed and consistent with the classic traditions of the mystery." Full cloth in dust jacket, $29.00. Trade softcover, $19.00.

Swords, Sandals And Sirens by Marilyn Todd.
Murder, conmen, elephants. Who knew ancient times could be such fun? Many of the stories feature Claudia Seferius, the super-bitch heroine of Marilyn Todd's critically acclaimed mystery series set in ancient rome. Others feature Cleopatra, the olympian gods, and high priestess Ilion blackmailed to work with Sparta's feared

secret police. Full cloth in dust jacket, signed and numbered by the author, $45.00. Trade softcover, $19.00.

The Puzzles of Peter Duluth by Patrick Quentin. Lost Classics Series.
Anthony Boucher wrote: "Quentin is particularly noted for the enviable polish and grace which make him one of the leading American fabricants of the murderous comedy of manners; but this surface smoothness conceals intricate and meticulous plot construction as faultless as that of Agatha Christie." Full cloth in dust jacket, $29.00. Trade softcover, $19.00.

Hunt in the Dark by Q. Patrick, Lost Classics Series. Full cloth in dust jacket, $29.00. Trade softcover, $19.00.

All But Impossible: The Impossible Files of Dr. Sam Hawthorne by Edward D. Hoch. Full cloth in dust jacket, signed and numbered by the publisher, $45.00. Trade softcover, $19.00.

Sequel to Murder by Anthony Gilbert, edited by John Cooper. Full cloth in dust jacket, $29.00. Trade softcover, $19.00.

Hildegarde Withers: Final Riddles? by Stuart Palmer with an introduction by Steven Saylor. Full cloth in dust jacket, $29.00. Trade softcover, $19.00

Shooting Script by William Link and Richard Levinson, edited by Joseph Goodrich. Full cloth in dust jacket, signed and numbered by the families, $47.00. Trade softcover, $22.00.

Subscriptions

Subscribers agree to purchase each forthcoming publication, either the Regular Series or the Lost Classics or (preferably) both. Collectors can thereby guarantee receiving limited editions, and readers won't miss any favorite stories.

Subscribers receive a discount of 20% off the list price (and the same discount on our backlist) and a specially commissioned short story by a major writer in a deluxe edition as a gift at the end of the year.

The point for us is that, since customers don't pick and choose which books they want, we have a guaranteed sale even before the book is published, and that allows us to be more imaginative in choosing short story collections to issue.

That's worth the 20% discount for us. Sign up now and start saving. Email us at orders@crippenlandru.com or visit our website at www.crippenlandru.com on our subscription page.

CPSIA information can be obtained
at www.ICGtesting.com
Printed in the USA
BVHW032245090123
655974BV00017B/85